THE CRIMSON WOLF

A Red Riding Hood Love Story

G.M. Fairy

CONTENT WARNING

The Crimson Wolf may not be suitable for all readers. For a full list of content warnings, please visit gmfairyauthor.com

To all the "knotty" bitches.

1

HOMECOMING

I try my best not to look at the wash of green streaming past my windows and focus on the road ahead. I grew up in these woods. You would think only five years away from them wouldn't make me forget their presence entirely, but I can't help it. Seeing so much greenery and nature holds a nostalgic feeling I cannot help but gawk at.

Someone honks from behind me, snapping me back to reality. I'm driving ten miles below the speed limit. They would have run me over in New York City by now, but I'm not in New York anymore. Nope. I'm at the city lines of Dayton, Washington—my hometown.

It's been too long since I've been home. I should have visited Granny more, but after graduating college and getting a job at the Times, there never was a break between stories. I've focused on accelerating my future, and revisiting my past was the least of my concerns. Granny has always understood. Although she constantly teased me about returning to visit her, she's always been my biggest supporter in following my dreams.

Granny's house sits only two minutes from the city limits, and before I know it, I'm pulling down her long driveway. The trees on either side of me connect overhead, making it seem like I'm driving through a tunnel. It worries me that she lives in such a desolate and hidden place. Obviously, it doesn't scare me enough to be a halfway decent granddaughter and visit her more often, but being busy enough can suck the decency right out of you.

When I reach the house, Granny jumps from her rocking chair on the porch, waving with a stained, toothy grin. Her white, puffy hair wobbles atop her head as she rushes toward me.

Everything looks the same as it did when I left five years ago. Ivy crawls up the stone walls. The foggy windows glow from the warm light inside, and the chimney spews a gray cloud of smoke from the burning hearth inside. Granny likes to keep the house warm, and with the constant wet and chill surrounding Washington, the fireplace always remains lit.

"Red," she squeals before wrapping me into a hug. For a woman so frail and tiny, her hugs are surprisingly intense. It's like the love inside of her is a superpower.

My name isn't actually Red, and no one besides the people from my hometown calls me that. In New York, everyone calls me by my middle name, Christine, but my birth certificate reads Mildred. And, of course, that's a horrible name, so I'll take Red any day of the week.

"Granny, I missed you." I try to match her hug but avoid squeezing too hard and hurting her.

"Let me take a look at you," she says as she puts me at arm's length. "Red, you're skin and bones. Are you even eating in New York?"

I shake my head. "I eat when I can. I've just been so busy with the new job."

"Ah, yes. The big reporter job at The New York Times. I can't wait to hear all about it. Come inside, and I'll make you some chicken and dumplings."

My mouth waters. Nothing tastes better than Granny's chicken and dumplings. It's basically better than sex, at least, as far as I remember sex. I haven't had time for anything for the past six months, not even a late-night booty call. God, why am I thinking about sex at my little old grandma's house? I shake my head and follow her inside her cottage.

As soon as I walk through the doorway, the familiar smells of my childhood hit me—cinnamon, sizzling onions, freshly cleaned laundry, and a slight hint of mothballs.

"Make yourself comfortable, and I'll finish up the food," Granny calls from the kitchen.

I carry my bags up to my bedroom. Everything looks the same as I left it. The quilted comforter lies on my twin-sized bed in the corner. My Hunger Games books have collected a line of dust on my bookshelf, but the pictures hanging on my wall look as clean as ever. I glance at the one of my parents and me at Disney World when I was four, my red hair looking unnatural compared to my faded surroundings. It was one of the last trips we took before they died. I sigh, still surprised that the thought of them stings. I've lived with Granny ever since then. She's the one who raised me and has loved me enough for two parents. The fact that their murder was so unnatural makes it all feel like an unhealed wound. That's probably why I've gotten into journalism and spend every waking second of my life trying to solve all the cases I can, like the one I'm here for.

"Red, food's ready!" Granny's voice knocks me out of my childhood trauma trance. I think that's the reason I hate coming back home. It's like seeing your childhood bedroom triggers my "I probably need to go to therapy" response, and I definitely don't have time for that.

I walk down the hall and into the kitchen, where Granny already has the pot of piping hot soup on top of her doily table center. I sit in my usual chair as she ladles the soup into the homemade ceramic bowl before me.

"So, how long are you staying for?" Granny asks as she takes her seat at the head of the table.

"Probably only a week. I just need to interview some law personnel and witnesses surrounding the attacks."

Granny shakes her head. "I reckon it will take longer than that. You know how everyone is in this town. People don't like to give out information to anyone. Especially when it doesn't put the town in a positive light."

I put my spoon down. "But I'm not just anyone. I grew up here. They'll talk to me."

Granny leans in and pinches my cheek. "You're not the same Red that ran away five years ago. I imagine people will scarcely recognize you besides your red hair and green eyes."

I shake my head. Although I lost some weight and have curves that betray my past self, I think Granny's being dramatic.

"Well, can you tell me anything about the attacks?"

"What's the hurry to find out so much? Enjoy your time while you're here." Granny picks up her bowl and heads to the sink.

"It's not that."

It is that.

"It's just that I have a deadline on this story. I only have two weeks to research *and* write the article. I need as much information as I can get."

Granny bustles around the table, tidying things up. "There's not much I can say. I just know those poor farmers were killed, and their bodies were found completely mangled in that strange circle. I know the same as everyone else." She stops what she's doing and pops up. "You know what! I think Jack was at the scene when they found the bodies. Maybe you should head to his hunting supply store tomorrow and ask him yourself."

My stomach drops. "Jack? As in Jack Lumberton?" He was my childhood best friend and also my childhood crush. The last time we saw each other, we didn't leave on the best terms. He's probably one of the reasons I haven't wanted to return. I do *not* want to talk to him tomorrow.

Granny gives me a knowing look. "I know there's a lot of history there, but maybe you can use that to your advantage. You two were always so close. He would probably be your best chance at giving you some good information. Besides, you're gonna want to see him. He grew up alright." Granny gives me a wink.

"Granny!" I squeal, unable to contain my laughter. She's always been a devilish flirt.

When my laughter subsides, I mentally weigh my options back and forth. I don't have any leads. All I have is that I grew up here, and I was so dreadfully shy that I doubt that would count for anything. Jack may be my only chance to get a start on this story. I shake my head. "Fine! I guess I'll see Jack before I head to the police station."

"Oh, goody!" Granny claps her hands like a young schoolgirl. I'll be sure to make you a hearty breakfast. I don't want you to faint once you run into him. I know I sure do almost every time I see him."

"Granny!" I squeal again, but my stomach drops. If what Granny is saying is true, maybe this isn't such a bright idea.

2

A BURLY PAST

The chime rings overhead as I swing open the door leading into "Jack's Tack and Co," a rustic log cabin with a wide wrap-around porch. It took forever to find this place, deep in the woods and down twisting dirt roads.

"Hello?" I call as I walk into the desolate store. The tiny shack didn't indicate they were open, but the door's unlocked, so I guess that's a good enough sign that I can enter.

I walk past a rack of fishing poles and examine a dusty box of bullets from the shelf to my left. Does anyone even shop here? It sure as hell doesn't look like it.

"Hello?" I call again. Silence.

Well, shit. How am I supposed to get answers if my best lead is MIA?

A bang comes from the back of the shop, snapping my attention away from the dusty merchandise. I shouldn't follow it. This is the exact scenario that every dumb bitch in a horror movie puts themself into before they get their head chopped off, but I'm a reporter. I have to go after the source. I follow the sound into a dimly lit back room. The bangs grow louder and more frequent with each step I take. Is it someone trapped in a cellar trying to get out? This is a cabin in the middle of nowhere—a perfect place to store captured victims.

My heart beats wildly as I lighten my footsteps and try to soften my breath. When I get to the end of the back room, I can see sunlight trickling in from an ajar door. The sound comes from outside. I follow it, pushing the door slightly.

An axe swings down, snapping a log in half. The shirtless man with tight brown pants, chopping the wood, swiftly picks up another log and puts it on the chopping block. The man is chiseled, muscles lining every inch of his sweaty frame. His jaw is lined with a full but tightly shaved crimson beard. His hazel-green eyes are intensely focused on chopping the wood before him.

I'm frozen in shock. I know this man. It's Jack, but it's also not Jack at all. Sure, he's always been tall, a staggering six foot three that seemed a little excessive since I'm barely pushing five foot three. But these muscles... He'd always been scrawny. I used to hate it because he could eat whatever he wanted while I ate a single fry and seemed to gain five pounds. He's definitely not scrawny anymore. Granny was right. I'm feeling a bit faint.

My palms must be sweating because my hand slips from the door frame, and I collapse to the floor, making the door swing wide open and hit a pile of wood neatly stacked next to it.

Jack snaps his attention to me. "Shit, are you okay?" He crouches over me, reaching for my hand to help me up.

Fuck, why does his sweat smell so good? It's like his pores ooze sandalwood and paprika. God, am I in a men's deodorant ad or something?

Our eyes catch, and his face looks as shocked as I feel. "Red?"

I reach for his arm, pulling myself up. "Yep," I grunt and stand, wiping my clamming hands on my jeans. "Sorry for the intrusion and," I turn to the pile of fallen logs, "the mess."

"Oh, it's fine." He waves his hand in dismissal. "Shit. Look at you. You look great! What has it been?"

"Five years," I say before he finishes. His eyes don't leave me—an intense look on his face. My mind races back to that night after graduation, before the earthquake.

He nods. "Yeah, I guess so."

My eyes trail from his face to his sweaty and muscular chest. I can't help it.

He notices this shift. "Oh, shit. Sorry." He turns and reaches for a red flannel on a log, pulling it over his shoulders. "So, what brings you into town and to my little shop of all places?"

I shake my head, returning my thoughts to my mission. "Yes, right. Well, I don't know if you know this, but I'm a reporter now at the Times."

"Yeah, I heard." He shakes his head. "I'm so proud of you." A longing look lingers in his eyes. "Let's go inside. It's a million degrees out here. I'll get you something to drink."

I part my lips to refuse. I just wanted to ask him my questions and get out of his way so it didn't turn into a bigger deal than it needed to be, but Jack doesn't give me a chance. He walks past me, back into his shop, leaving me with no option but to follow after him.

He ventures down a small hallway to his right, away from the shop entrance. It leads to a living room with a fireplace and two comfortable-looking armchairs. "Have a seat. Can I get you water, tea, coffee?" He motions to the chairs but walks to the small kitchen at the other end of the room.

"Do you live here?" I question as I look around the space.

Jack calls from the kitchen, already pulling out two mugs and making coffee on the stove. "Yeah. Remember my Uncle Jerry? Well, he died four years back and left me this cabin. I decided to turn it into a store and live here."

"Oh, I'm sorry about his passing." I take a seat on the flannel armchair closest to me. I've interviewed hundreds of witnesses before, meeting them at their houses or various locations. I usually am calm and in control of the situation, but right now, it feels like my heart might beat out of my chest. This isn't just any eye-witness. This is Jack, and here I am in his little cottage in the middle of the woods as he makes me a cup of coffee, using his ungodly muscles to do so. *God, those muscles*. How can I think of anything else?

"It's okay. We were never that close. I was just his only nephew, and he had no kids."

"How's your dad?" I call.

"Dead."

"Oh, Jack, I'm so sorry." I want to punch myself.

"It's alright. You know how my old man and I never really got along. He was never the same after my mom died."

Jack and I bonded over both having dead parents growing up. He still had his dad, but now I guess we're even. His father was a cold man—spitting image of Jack, but never cracked a smile. The two were always arguing, which made me thankful to grow up with such a loving Granny.

I search my memories for the details of his mother's death. She was murdered, much like my parents. Back then, I didn't reflect on the similarities much, but now...

Jack interrupts my thoughts, emerging from his kitchen, holding two cups of coffee in white diner mugs. I reach out and take the one he offers me. "How did you know I wanted coffee? You didn't even give me a chance to answer your question?"

His hazel eyes hold mine as if he's sucking in the deepest parts of me. "I know you, Red. You're never one to turn down coffee." He sits in the seat across from me and brings the cup up to his lips, his eyes never leaving mine.

I look down at my mug, trying to find a distraction from the buzzing taking over my body. "That's pretty assumptious of you. A lot about me has changed since I left."

"I see that, but I can tell what matters has stayed the same."

I shake my head. I'm not letting him distract me like he did for most of my life. No matter what he says, I'm a different woman now. My life doesn't revolve around him and his opinions of me.

I take out my recorder, flip it on, and hold it up. "So, Jack, I'm here because of the attacks. I'm reporting on the case and in a bit of a time crunch. I heard you were one of the first people on the scene."

Jack looks down at his mug and takes in a big breath. A moment of silence passes as I wait for him to respond. He finally returns my gaze. "Have you been to the old diner since you've been back? It looks exactly the same as when we used to go."

I squint my eyes. "What?"

"Joanne's Diner. You know, the one we used to go to every Friday after the games. Come on now, don't tell me the five years away has made you forget everything!"

Is he seriously trying to avoid my question? This is so like him. He's always had a habit of letting me down when I need him most. "Jack, the attack. Can you tell me about it?"

He sighs. "Everything was already in the news. There isn't anything else for me to tell."

I know he's lying. Not even because I've known him my whole life and can tell from the way his eyebrows pinch together, he's avoiding the question. There's something he doesn't want to tell me. But why? This just confirms my suspicion that this isn't just some freak animal attack.

I breathe out and soften my expression. "Jack, please. I don't have many options. I really care about my job." My puppy dog eyes have always worked in the past to get men to answer questions or to cut corners to find out more about a story. The art of seduction is one I've mastered well in the past five years, but I've never used it on Jack before, and this just feels all kinds of wrong.

Jack's reaction is palpable. He stares at me with parted lips. His shoulders tighten, and his breath heavies.

I can't deny that having this effect on him has been the source of every wet dream of my teenage years. Except it's a little too late and stings too much. He sure does know how to make all my wildest dreams come true at the worst time. I clear my throat and stiffen, looking away from Jack's intense stare.

He's knocked out of his trance and sits up straight, tugging at the collar of his flannel. "How about this? Why don't I take you to dinner tomorrow night, and we can discuss more?"

"Tomorrow? I'm kind of on a time crunch. Can't we just talk now?"

"I know it's hard for you to believe, but I also have a job. I have work to do, and the next time I'm available is tomorrow night."

I'm about to protest. I saw his shop. It doesn't look like he's had a customer in years. What could he possibly need to do from now until tomorrow night? But then I realize Jack is one of my only sources. Granny was right. It will be like pulling teeth to get anyone else to talk to me, and who would be a better witness than the person who showed up to the scene first?

"Fine." I barely catch myself saying it. "We'll have dinner, as friends, and then you'll tell me everything you know." I stand up.

Jack chuckles. "Sure, as friends, and then we'll see what happens."

I give him an incredulous look. What the fuck does that mean? I don't want to spend all day bickering with him, though. It's already bringing up too many memories from my past as it is. I walk toward the hallway from where we came, but Jack grabs my hand before I get very far. Electricity shoots down my body, and I have to stop myself from shuttering. I turn to face him. His eyes capture mine, and we stand in silence for a moment.

"What?" I finally manage to stutter.

He releases his grasp and runs his large hand through his crimson hair. "I'll pick you up at seven. At Granny's."

"Oh, yeah. Right." I charge toward the exit, fighting the urge to glance back at him as I leave. I'm a changed woman now. He can't have this effect on me. Except I know that's a lie. He obviously still can.

Jesus Christ, this story is going to be harder than I thought.

3

WHAT CREEPS IN THE NIGHT

Lighting bursts around me, and my eyes shoot open. Rain pelts my bare skin, and a chill seeps deep into my bones. I sit up, holding my chest to protect my nakedness from the harsh elements. A scream rises from my belly as I glance at the dead bodies piled around me, their necks bloodied and their eyes forever blank.

"Help!" I yell, feeling the creeping doom that I'm the next victim of whatever beast killed these people.

Although the faces of the dead raise bile from my stomach, I can't look away, an unexplainable urge to search for someone taking over.

A gargled scream escapes me when I see them, and I run over to their pale and lifeless bodies. My parents. Just as young and beautiful as I remember them from when I was a child. My mother's golden blonde hair is pristine among the gore and filth. My father is clean-shaven and unblemished, and his golden-brown hair is smoothly kept. They lie beside each other on top of the heap of bodies, their hands intertwined.

I lean over them, feeling all the longing and despair as I did so long ago. I'm a little girl again, abandoned and hopeless. Except I'm not. I'm a twenty-three-year-old woman, just with all the fresh pain of my youth.

My sobs are knocked out of my chest by a low and powerful growl penetrating through the rain. I bolt to my feet, peering through the storm and forest.

Amber eyes peer at me through the darkness, circling me. Shadows and brush hide the dark figure hosting these eyes. I try to follow them as it moves around me, not wanting the creature to rush upon me from behind, but it's too fast. It almost seems as if multiple creatures are stalking me, but the amber eyes look the same—powerful and ready to devour me.

The figure walks closer to me, and my naked skin flushes with goosebumps. Terror grips around my heart, increasing to jackrabbit speed. As it gets closer, I can make out its size. It's a beast crawling on all fours. The size of it is unnatural. I still can't distinguish its features through the pelting rain and darkness.

The creature is out of sight in the blink of an eye, but its hot breath feathers the back of my neck. Large human hands wrap around my middle, trailing slowly up and down my bare skin. Something inside of me warms. The beast's breath trails down my neck, inhaling my scent. A scream rests at the tip of my lips, begging to release, but I will myself to silence—knowing there's no use. The beast growls low and pulls me against him—the hardness of his body enveloping me.

My blood thickens, and my breath heavies. Terror is prevalent in my veins, but it's not all I feel. Right at the base, there's a longing. A longing for his hands to explore more of me. To turn around and capture those magnetic eyes with mine. To be devoured by the beast until there's nothing left of me. My breath hitches in anticipation.

The beast brings his lips back to my ear. "Don't run. You belong to me." His silky black voice sears deep into my soul.

My nerves gather up, braveness replacing them, and I will myself to turn and face him, but when I do, he's gone. In his place is a flash of lightning, throwing me back to the forest floor.

***

I jolt up, my limbs tangled in my white sheets, sweat lining every inch of my skin. The walls shake around me. My lungs heave in my chest as I take inventory of my childhood room and my grey pajama set soaked in sweat. It was a dream. Only a dream.

"Red! You okay!" Granny yells from across the hall.

"Yes!" I call back. The picture frames rattle on the wall. "Are you okay?"

"Yes, just a tiny earthquake. It's funny; they only seem to happen when you're here."

The movement stops, but a storm rages outside, heavy raindrops pelting against my window.

"I think we're good. Goodnight!" she yells. My Granny's probably the only person in existence to be so nonchalant about an earthquake. The last one I experienced was the night of graduation five years ago—the night my heart ripped in two, and I vowed to stay far away from this place.

She's rubbed off on me because my mind quickly flips from the earthquake to my dream. I bring my hand to my chest, trying to will my heart to slow down. My core heats as I recount the details of my nightmare. The feeling alarms me. What the fuck is wrong with me? How could such a disturbing dream make me so horny?

I pick up my phone on my nightstand. It's three a.m. I have a busy day ahead of me, ending with dinner with Jack. I need a full night of sleep to stand a chance of having my bearings while with him.

I slam back down in my bed, snapping my eyes shut and willing myself to turn off my brain and fall back asleep. But even I can't deny the part of me that secretly hopes I'll be taken back to where my dream left off—to the beast that promised to destroy me.

4

NEW FRIENDS

"Well, that was a big fucking waste of time!" I yell to myself as I slam my body down on the park bench outside the police station. Even though I'm having dinner with Jack tonight, I figured it would be good to talk to the local police and see what they could tell me. After only fifteen minutes of being gaslighted and rushed out of the station, I'm left with more questions. There's something they don't want me to know. That or Granny was right about people in this town not trusting outsiders.

Most of the officers I'd grown up with, even though they gave no indication that they'd seen me before. Sergeant Brick was the man I thought could give me the answers. He was a new face, a handsome face, actually, with greyish-brown hair and grey, piercing eyes. I hoped he'd have less loyalty to the town's secrets. I was wrong. That man was as stubborn as his name suggests. I wasn't getting any answers. I guess my only hope now is Jack.

I sigh, digging through my bag and pulling out my phone. Two missed calls from my editor. *Fuck.*

I quickly call her back.

"Hello?" Angela's crisp voice sounds from the other side of the phone.

"Hi, Angela. I'm sorry I missed your calls. I was at the Dayton Police Station trying to find out more."

"And?" Her voice rises over the commotion in the background.

I glance around at the expanse of the green park before me. I imagine our settings couldn't be more different. I want nothing more than to be back in the hustle and bustle of the office. It's too goddamn quiet here.

"They told me it was nothing but a freak accident, that the case has already been closed."

She huffs. "You'd think they'd have a better excuse than that. If anything, that makes everything more suspicious."

"That's what I thought."

"So what next? I put you on this story because you have connections there."

"I do. I'm meeting with an old friend for dinner tonight. I think he might know something. Is there any way I can get an extension on this? I'm not sure I can get everything done in a week."

She sighs, silent for a moment as if contemplating. "Yeah, sure, why not. I don't think the higher-ups are even interested in this story."

Fuck, I didn't expect it to be that easy. Maybe I'm less valuable to the team than I thought. "Oh, well, I think we got something here. In fact, I don't need an extra week. I can hurry and work through the nights."

"Don't worry about it. Enjoy yourself. Come back when you're ready. You know how slow news is during the summers anyways."

"No, really, Angela. I want to work. I'll get the story back to you as soon as I can."

"Whatever. Alright, talk to you later." She hangs up.

"Fuck," I say, cradling my phone in my hand.

"Work giving you crap?" A woman's voice startles me. I look over at the short-haired brunette sitting next to me. She slides closer. "Uh, yeah." I give a tight-lipped smile, looking back at my phone on my lap.

"Tell me about it. I work at Joanne's Diner, and my boss makes me want to commit murder most of the time." She smiles, leaning back, her silver nose ring catching in the sunlight.

"Oh, yeah. I used to go there all the time. I'm meeting a friend there tonight, actually."

She hits my arm harder than I think she means to. I rub at the spot. "No, shit! I'll see you there. I'm working tonight." I notice the light trail of freckles under her green eyes. "Where do you work?" she asks.

"The Times."

"As in the New York Times?"

"That's the one."

"Well, shit. What are you doing here?" She pulls her legs onto the park bench and turns to me. This girl has never met a stranger.

"I grew up here, but I'm here to investigate those bodies found in the clearing."

She jumps to her feet. "Fuck yes! Finally, someone is going to do something about it. I've been coming to the police station every day to get those jackasses to make some moves, but they're too chicken shit."

"Do you know the people that were murdered?" I flip on my recorder in my pocket.

Her shoulders sag, and her eyes dart from left to right. "Yeah, they were people in my community." I've known this girl for a total of five minutes, but I can tell she's holding something back.

I nod. "I'm part of this community too. Well, I used to be. Those people don't look familiar to me."

"What's your name?" she asks, sitting back down and leaning closer to me. "I don't think I've ever seen you around."

"Red Hoodson. I look a little different than when I..."

"Hoodson?" she yells. "I knew your dad!"

"You did?" She looks about my age, and I was five when he died. Maybe she's a few years older than me, though.

"Yeah, he was the old park ranger. I was just a kid, but I remember him."

I nod. "Yeah, he was."

"I'm so sorry to hear what happened to him." The light from her eyes dim.

I exhale. "It's alright. I was five when they died. I barely even knew them."

She shakes her head, leaning back and looking at the park. "This town has a habit of letting bad things slide. I'm fucking sick of it."

"Well, that's why I'm here." I lean closer, holding out my recorder. "Is there anything you can think of to help me put the pieces together?"

She looks nervously down at the recorder before meeting my eyes again. "What you need is to get that dick in there to do something about it."

"Sergeant Brick?"

"That's the one! He won't even see me, and I know it's just because I fucked two of his officers."

I can't help but laugh. "What?"

She smacks her lips and smiles. "What? It's a small town. Who else am I supposed to fuck?"

I nod. "Touche." I like this girl.

She looks down at her wristwatch. "Shit. I gotta get going. I'm working a double today." She stands. "It was good to meet ya! Hopefully, I'll see you around, and you can scare these dickwads into doing something about this."

"Oh, I never got your name," I call after her.

"Carmen! Carmen Badson."

"Good to meet you!"

She salutes before turning and walking away.

Maybe this morning had been a waste, but at least I made a friend. Maybe making friends is the secret to getting answers around here.

5

DINERS AND OTHER DISASTERS

"Fuck!" I yell as I trip over my overflowing duffle bag on my floor. I've spent the last two hours going through everything I brought with me in an attempt to find something suitable to wear tonight. We're going to our small-town's country diner, for Christ's sake. Most people don't even change out of their sweatpants, but for some reason, I feel an unexplainable urge to impress Jack, which calls for a more appealing outfit. Of course, the urge isn't *that* unexplainable. He's my childhood best friend and crush, and to make matters worse, he's grown even more insatiably hot over the past five years. I'm thinking with my vagina that, if we're being honest, hasn't had much action in the last year. It's hard to date when your job is all-consuming, and I've never felt the need for a long-term relationship.

And then there was last night's dream. I didn't think it was possible to be hornier than I was once I left Jack's shop, but after waking from my unusually terrifying and arousing nightmare, I found it hard to fall back asleep. Being in my childhood home with the foreboding news of recent death and carnage must be taking a toll on my subconscious. Mix that in with my dire need to get laid—a recipe for fucked up nightmares.

Last night, the thought of caring for the pounding between my thighs in my childhood bed with my little old Granny down the hall was enough to keep my wandering fingers at bay. But now here I am, frazzled and horny, about to go on a date with the last person I ever wanted to see again when I left five years ago.

Well, I shouldn't say date. It's not a date. This is for business only. That's it.

I'm a terrible liar, though, even to myself. I saw the way Jack looked at me, the way he almost seemed to be bribing me to go to dinner with him. He behaved in a way that my teenage self could only dream of. For some reason, this makes it hurt even worse. It's a little too late for that. He has always had the worst timing.

As if fate hears my thoughts, Granny calls up the stairs. "Red, Jack is here!"

"Fuck," I mutter again as I stare at my reflection in my floor-length mirror. My red hair is still in curlers, and all I'm wearing is my lacey black bra and denim high-waisted jeans.

"I'll be down in five minutes!" I yell toward my door before scrambling to yank out the curlers in my hair and search my bedroom floor for a halfway decent shirt.

After more like fifteen minutes, I settle on a plain white tank top and descend the stairs.

Granny's full-belly laugh greets me before I'm even close enough to see her in the kitchen. She and Jack sit knee to knee at the dining room table. Jack hunches over, divulging a tale that has Granny wiping away tears and at the edge of her seat.

When I reach the last step, the old floorboards creak beneath me, and Jack's focus whips to me. The smile slowly melts off his face, replaced by a longing gaze. His stare makes my stomach flip-flop, and I'm brought back to my old self, who never knew what to say.

"Don't you look nice!" Granny exclaims like an angel from heaven, breaking Jack and me out of whatever trance we found ourselves in. I can't help but notice a shift in Granny. Her eyes seemed glazed over and blood-shot, even if an all-teeth smile takes up most of her face.

Jack jumps up from his seat. "Yeah, you look wonderful."

"Thanks," I reply noncommittally. I'm wearing a tank top and jeans. It's not like I came down the stairs to greet them in my prom dress. No, Jack never let me have that moment.

Granny wobbles over to me and kisses my cheek, lingering to whisper in my ear. "See, what did I tell ya? He's a smoke show!"

"Granny!" I whisper in embarrassment. Surely, Jack can hear us.

He grins and turns his gaze to the floor, confirming my suspicion. He rubs at his muscular forearm, further accentuated by his tight-fitting black t-shirt.

I shake my head, catching myself staring. "Well, we should get going." I walk toward the front door, not looking behind me to see if he's following. This already feels too much like a date, and it hasn't even officially started.

"You two have fun!" Granny calls after us as I walk out the front door, Jack at my heels.

***

After a short and uncomfortably awkward car ride, we make it to Joanne's Diner. Jack was right. The old diner is *exactly* the same as it was five years ago, down to the duct-taped women's restroom sign. It's nice to see something that reminds me of mostly fond childhood memories, but being put back in the headspace of my sixteen-year-old self is a bit unnerving.

"Seat yourself!" a waitress yells from behind the counter.

"To our usual seat?" Jack turns to me and motions to the booth closest to the door. Unsurprisingly, it's empty. That's why it was our booth growing up. No one wants to sit next to the door that's always opening and closing, and growing up, we were too thrilled to have our own personal seat to care. Now I'm an adult, though—a New Yorker—many things bother me. One is the constant wind hitting the back of my neck as I eat.

"Sure." I lead the way to the red booth. I need something from Jack. The more I can get on his good side, the better.

"Hiya, friend!" I turn to Carmen. Her short hair is pulled behind her ears, and she's wearing a blue apron. She slides sticky plastic menus in front of us.

"Hi!" I smile. "This is Jack."

"Ms. Badson." He doesn't meet her eyes, and his tone holds a sharp edge.

"Lumberton," she replies with the same edge.

"You two know each other?" I ask.

"Barely," Jack mutters.

She scoffs.

It is a small town. Maybe they fucked. I, for one, do not want to dig up those details. An awkward silence passes between us.

"Drinks?" She pulls out her notepad without looking up at us.

"Yes. I'll have a Coke and Red over here, will have a strawberry milkshake."

"Wait, no." I give him a confused look. "I'll just have a water."

Jack looks at me as if I just told him I hate puppies and sunshine.

Carmen rolls her eyes and wanders off without another word.

"But you always got the strawberry milkshake. I thought you would want one for old time's sake." Confusion and hurt flood his eyes.

I pull the menu to my line of vision and pretend to examine my options. "Well, I told you, a lot about me has changed." I don't want to mention that I've written off milkshakes ever since I moved away from here and vowed to shed my unwanted weight. It's too depressing to mention.

An uncomfortable silence rolls between us, but thankfully, it doesn't take long for Carmen to come back over with our drinks. She pulls out her notepad again. "What can I get ya?"

I speak up first this time. "I'll have the chef's salad." I slide my menu to her. "Thank you." I smile, hoping she doesn't hate me for associating with Jack.

Jack shakes his head without looking up from his menu. "I'll have the bacon burger with fries."

"Just give me a few minutes, and I'll be right out with that." She smiles and winks at me, then disappears, leaving us with nothing to distract ourselves with.

"The chef's salad, really?" He shakes his head at me. "No one gets the chef's salad."

I'm about to snap. Sure, he would think getting the chef's salad is ridiculous. He doesn't have an ounce of fat on him, and he never has. I, on the other hand, seem to gain weight just thinking about food. It hasn't been a concern since moving to New York and walking everywhere, but I'm not in New York right now. I'm in the middle of nowhere, completely surrounded by fast-food restaurants. I breathe out, deciding to ignore his idiotic comment and focus on the matter at hand.

I fold my hands in front of me. "So, Jack. What can you tell me about what you saw at the scene of the attacks?"

He takes a long sip of his drink but still gazes at me. "You know, you're really beautiful."

My heart stops. "What?"

"I just realized I haven't told you that in a while. You've always been beautiful, and it's just so good to see you again."

I can't help how my body melts into my seat, and I'm finding breathing impossible. This isn't the first time he's told me something like this, but as always, it's at the worst possible time. The tingly feeling in my limbs is quickly replaced by rage. He's trying to distract me. He's always known the effect he has on me.

I shake my head. "Jack, let's not do this."

"Do what?"

Before I can say more, Carmen comes back over with our food. Damn, the food comes out fast here. This diner has never been known for its fine dining. They probably just zap it in the microwave.

"Enjoy," she says after plopping down our entrees and sauntering away.

I look at my wilted salad and see why people rarely order salads here. I try to find the words to respond to Jack. "Jack, I'm here for work. I need to learn more about these attacks, and I know you know more than you're letting on. I'm really not in the mood to flirt or entertain the past. It's too painful and in the way of what I'm trying to accomplish."

He sighs and gives a wounded nod before biting his burger. "Maybe you're right. Maybe you have changed." He says once he's finished chewing.

I nod and pick at my salad, waiting for him to say more. When he doesn't, I speak up again. "Well?"

"I don't know what you want me to say. I can't..." He stops himself, looking like he's trying to find the right words.

"Jack, you told me if I came here with you, you'd tell me more. Don't tell me that you were just fucking with my head."

"Red, I missed you. I wanted a chance to talk more—to go over everything that happened before you left. I think about it all the time."

I bolt up from my seat. "No. I'm not doing this. I'm here for work. If you won't help me get more answers about this story, I'll do it myself." I turn to walk away.

"Wait, Red. It's dangerous."

I stop in my tracks, wanting to ask him to explain himself, but before I do, I shake my head and walk out the door. I knew there was more to this story than he was letting on. If it's dangerous, that means there's an interesting story to tell–and I *will* be the one to tell it.

6

THE BEAST

It's always raining in Washington, so I don't know why it's a shock to me as I pull my rental car up to the edge of the woods and discover I'm stuck in a rainstorm. This is stupid. I don't need to investigate the crime scene right now, alone in the middle of a downpour, but I have adrenaline and anger rushing through my veins. It's like there's some internal alarm blaring to see the scene for myself. I don't need a man to help me uncover this case, especially not Jack. Yeah, I'm pretty sure he knows something—something he doesn't want me to find out, but I'd rather discover it myself than muddy up our past.

I grab the raincoat from the backseat of my car and pull it over me before stepping out. Luckily, I have a flashlight to guide me through the small and overgrown trail of the forest. I knew that the place they found the bodies wasn't too far away from Jack's cabin, but as I pass it in the distance, it's all too apparent to me how he is somehow connected to this. I feel it in my bones.

Thunder cracks in the distance overhead, and I jump. I've never been one to frighten easily, but there is apparently a murderous beast hiding in these woods, and I'm putting myself in the perfect position to be its next meal. God, I'm an idiot. But I'm already too deep in the woods to head back. Something calls me deeper and deeper, making me ignore reason. Maybe it's the reporter in me urging me to take matters into my own hands, or maybe it's something more, some instinctual ability. It's like there's a tiny force pulling me along.

I come to a clearing—a clearing that I suspect was the place they discovered the bodies based on the leftover crime scene tape trampled around me. Of course, there's no sign of the carnage. They had carted away the bodies weeks ago.

I don't know what I'm looking for. It's not like I can see much through the wash of rain anyway. If anything, being here may help me paint a better picture of the scene in my write-up. At least if I can't find anything else about this story, I can write a good exposition piece.

I point my flashlight toward the ground, searching for footprints or leftover evidence. Just when I'm about to give up, I see something. I kneel to the ground, letting the rain pelt against my back. In the dirt is a fresh footprint. You'd think the rain would melt it away, but it's huge, the size of two of my hands—leaving a crater in the earth.

A chill runs down my spine. This isn't like any animal print I've seen before. I'm not an expert in tracks, but I know this isn't natural. I have to get out of here, but just when the urgent thought pops into my head, a low and deep growl sounds from behind me.

I jump to my feet and turn around, pointing my flashlight toward the noise. There's not much visible through the rain and darkness, but the glow of bright yellow eyes is almost blinding.

I want to scream, but I know that will just startle the creature more. There's nothing I can do. I'm defenseless and alone in the middle of the woods with a supernatural animal.

Something barrels through the woods to the right of the glowing-eyed figure. I still can't make out the creature entirely, but it seems to be thrown down by something much larger. I can't make out the gold eyes anymore, but I can see the evidence of a tussle. If there's a creature more frightening than the one belonging to those eyes, I'm really in trouble. A creature whimpers and then runs away from the clearing, the sound of mighty footsteps crunching on the ground farther away. But there's a sound of a second set of footsteps heading closer toward me.

I hold my breath, grabbing a branch next to me as a pathetic attempt to protect myself from whatever is coming my way—whatever scared away the beast. The rain softens, and I can see more clearly. As the figure gets closer, its size becomes apparent. It's not a creature at all but a man—an enormous man.

7

ENORMOUS DANGER

"What the hell are you doing out here?" I hear his deep voice before I can see him, but the rain continues to clear, and the man gets closer, allowing me to make out his features.

"Hello? Do you have a death wish? What are you doing here?" He's right in front of me, staring me down with eyes so dark they're like black holes sucking me in.

I can't find the words to respond; they're stuck at the back of my throat.

The enormous stranger towers over me. His jet-black hair is slicked back, and water drips from his angular features. God, he's the most devastating man I've ever seen. A rush of energy zips through my veins, and my skin suddenly feels too tight for my body. I place my hand over my chest, wondering if this must be what it's like to come down from adrenaline.

"Hello! Earth to the dumb girl alone in the woods! Do you hear me?"

Apparently, he's an enormous asshole. Figures, the hot ones always are.

I snap out of my daze. "Yes, I can hear you! What am I doing here? I have the same right to be here as you. I could ask you the same question."

He stands steps away from me, and his eyes lock on mine. His pupils dilate, his nostrils expand, and his chest heaves as if not only am I an annoyance but also the most disgusting thing he's ever smelt. He chuckles and wipes his mouth with the back of his hand before turning his head and taking a deep breath. Why is he acting like this conversation is torture? I'm the one who's getting berated.

"It's my job to be out here. I'm the park ranger. Now, what are you doing here?" This time, his tone isn't as harsh.

"You're a park ranger?" He doesn't look like any park ranger I've ever seen. I examine him from head to toe. He's wearing a white t-shirt, completely see-through, revealing his chiseled chest and stomach, and black jeans—not exactly what I would think the uniform would be for a National Park Ranger.

He must catch me staring because he spins around and faces me with his arms outstretched. "Did you get a good enough look?"

God, he's an asshole. "You just do not look like a park ranger."

He smacks his lips and gives an agitated laugh. "And now tell me, what do park rangers look like?"

I stutter. "I don't know. Looser, non-see-through clothes, maybe a badge, a dorky hat."

"Well, I'm sorry to disappoint you with my attire, but I'm not sure you have any room to judge." He motions his gaze down to my chest.

I look down at my white tank top, completely soaked and revealing my lacy black bra. "Excuse me!" I yell in horror as I wrap my arms around my chest.

"I'm just pointing out the hypocrisy in your slut shaming." He pulls a carton from his pocket and brings a cigarette to his lips. The rain has completely stopped, allowing him to light it, even as water drips from his forehead. "Now, to direct you back to my initial question. Why the hell are you out here in a storm? Didn't you hear about the attacks that happened out here? Are you trying to get yourself killed? Do I need to call a suicide hotline?"

"Actually, that's why I'm here! I work for the New York Times, and I'm here to investigate the attacks."

He gives a disgusted chuckle. "Oh, figures. I knew I could smell a vulture. Can't you just let the families heal in peace? Why must you dig your nose where it doesn't belong?"

I've never condoned violence, but right now, I could ruin this guy's pretty little face. I'm surprised he's managed to keep it intact with a mouth like that.

"Look, I'm not here telling you that you shouldn't be doing your job. Besides, people need to be aware of the truth. The truth makes people safe. You know damn well there's nothing normal about those attacks, and it's becoming more and more apparent to me that something is going on here."

He's silent for a moment, which is surprising since he hasn't stopped berating me in the last five minutes since I've met him.

"You're wrong," he finally says.

"Oh, I am?"

"Yes. You said you're not telling me I shouldn't be doing my job when, in fact, you are here arguing with me instead of leaving like I asked."

"You never asked me to leave! You just asked me why I was here."

He scoffs. "You know what? You're right. I apologize. Please get the hell out of here. Thank you." He smiles at me, and I have to stop myself from slamming my fist into those pearly whites. God, his smile is like something from a toothpaste commercial.

"Fine. I'm leaving, but I will be back." I walk toward the edge of the clearing and fish around in my pockets for my keys. I stop in my tracks. "Shit." It starts raining again as if God is playing some cruel joke on me.

"What?"

I turn back to him, surprised that he's still standing in the spot I left him in.

"Nothing." I look around on the ground and trail back to where I examined the footprint. "It's just... my keys."

He laughs. "Of course, you lost your keys."

"What's that supposed to mean?" I whip around, my soaking wet red hair slapping me in the face.

"I've just known you for five minutes and can already read you like a book."

I drop my hands, feeling utterly defeated. "What is your problem? I don't even know you. Why are you being so mean?" Tears push at my eye ducts, and I turn around before he can see my tears. I'm not usually the type to get emotional, but this whole day has been a whirl of emotions. Between thinking I'm going to be eaten alive to being completely disappointed in men—I can't take it anymore.

He sighs and remains silent for a moment. He must notice I'm crumbling because his tone softens. "Look, I'm sorry, okay. I don't deal with people often, and you almost got hurt, and I don't like when people get hurt in my woods."

I breathe in, trying to stall my tears. I must admit, his half-assed apology softens the sting of the day just a tiny bit.

The rain pelts harder.

"You're not going to find your keys in this weather. Why don't you just come back to my place, and you can call someone to pick you up?"

"No thanks." I continue my search on the ground. I'm already dirty and completely soaked. Why worry about the rain?

Lightning cracks overhead.

Great.

I stand up and sigh. "Fine, but just to let you know, I am experienced in Krav Maga. Try anything, and I'll kick your ass."

He gives a genuine chuckle, and honestly, it lightens my sour mood a little more. "I don't doubt you will."

He leads me down a trail through the woods.

And for some asinine reason, I follow.

8

DARK STRANGER

The enormous asshole of a man leads me to a small cottage about a mile away from the clearing. What's with all the hot men in this town living in the middle of the woods? Hopefully, it's not to murder unsuspecting women caught in a rainstorm.

He opens the wooden door for me but doesn't enter. "The phone is on the wall by the kitchen." He takes a seat on the rocking chair on the porch and lights another cigarette.

"You don't have a cellphone?" I ask before stepping inside. I'd much rather him just bring it out to me so I don't have to go into this stranger's house. He could probably strangle me without even using much force. His hands are as massive as the rest of his body.

"It's dead." He looks out toward the woods and rocks in his chair.

I don't move. I know it's an idiotic idea to step into this stranger's house, but what other choice do I have? Besides, if he wanted to murder me so badly, would he make so much of an effort to save my life from whatever beast he scared away in the woods? I mean, maybe he just wanted to kill me himself, but I need some hope if I ever plan on making it home.

The stranger looks at me from the corner of his eye. "I'll stay out here, and you can make your call," he says as if reading my thoughts.

"Thanks." This calms my nerves a bit, and before I can think about it too much, I step inside and charge toward the old-timey phone hanging on the kitchen wall.

My heart beats wildly as the phone rings, and I gaze around the small living quarters. Although the outside of the cottage looks old and rustic, the inside holds a more modern flair besides the giant, antique-looking windows. He has stainless steel appliances, a flat-screen TV, a leather couch, a record player with an extensive vinyl collection, and...

My heart drops to my stomach once I notice the handcuffs and chains attached to a wooden pillar at the far end of the room. Shit. This guy *is* a serial killer.

"Hello?" Granny's frail voice knocks me out of my terrified trance.

I put my hand to the receiver, trying to muffle my words so the murderer doesn't hear me from outside. "Granny, it's me. Can you come pick me up? I'm at some crazy guy's house in the middle of the woods. I lost my car keys."

"Woah, Red, calm down! Where are you?"

"I'm not sure. I'm at a cabin near where they found all the bodies from the attack."

"Isn't that where Jack lives? Let me call him. He can pick you up."

"Wait, no..." The line clicks off, leaving me with an insistent buzz.

I redial Granny's number, but it's busy. She must have got a hold of Jack. *Great.*

"Everything okay?" The floorboards creak, and the enormous man steps through the door frame, ducking his head as he enters.

I drop the phone. "Shit. Sorry. Yeah, everything's fine. My big, strong boyfriend should be here any second."

The stranger no longer enters the house; he just watches me from the frame. He nods. "Okay." I can't help but notice his shoulders sagging and his forehead pinching. I bet he's disappointed he won't get me long enough to dispose of my body.

I pick up the phone from the floor and attach it back to its wall holder, my heart beating out of my chest.

"Can I get you anything?"

"No!" I yell, immediately regretting the terror in my voice. "I'm fine. I'll just sit out with you on the porch."

"Okay." He doesn't move. "Are you sure you're okay?"

I can't help it; my eyes flash to the chains in the corner.

He follows my gaze and runs his hand through his short, dark hair, revealing the underside of his muscular forearm. "Oh, shit." He laughs. "I guess that looks a bit terrifying. As a park ranger, I take care of any injured animals I find. Some of them are dangerous, much like the wolf you almost met in the clearing. Those chains are to protect me and the animal before I can get more help."

Wolf? So that's what he's calling that creature I saw in the clearing. I know for damn sure it was the size of a car, but now that I think of it, my fear could have dramatized the size.

"Why do you chain the animals inside your house?" The boldness of my voice surprises me. I'm dealing with a suspected murderer, yet my mind can't help but wonder if he's just the person who would have the answers to the mystery of the attacks unless he's the culprit. Sure, the reports indicated that the wounds were from animals, but a man of his size could make it look that way.

"They're injured. If I leave them outside, other animals will attack them." He steps closer, and I step to the side, trying to get around him.

"Surely your station would have a better place to keep injured animals." My dad was a park ranger, but I don't know shit about where they work. They never seemed to have *take your kids to work day* during the first five years of my life.

"Station?" He scrunches his thick eyebrows and chuckles.

We're both taking slow steps, him toward me, me toward the door.

"Yeah, doesn't the Department of Parks have a home base or something?"

"You're looking at it." He extends his arms and motions to the space around him. "You're looking at a department of one."

"You are the only park ranger in Dayton?" I had always assumed my dad had co-workers back then.

"You must be new. This town isn't known for its size."

I'm now steps away from the door. "I'm not new. I grew up here."

His steps track mine, and he wags his finger. "I knew you looked familiar. What's your name?"

"You don't look familiar."

He chuckles and rubs the back of his head. "Fair. I did stay pretty secluded growing up."

I really don't care about carrying on this conversation. "Cool." I slip outside of the door and rush down his porch, my heart pounding out of my chest.

"Hey, wait. Where are you going?" he calls from behind me, following me out.

"I told you, my big, strong boyfriend is picking me up. I don't want him to get lost." I'm trying not to look like I'm running, but I'm moving fast, almost toward the edge of his clearing.

Suddenly, I'm whipped back around. My heart hammers as I look up at the stranger holding my arm. I don't know how he got to me so fast.

Terror swims through my veins, but somehow, being this close to him makes me unable to look away. I get lost in his dark eyes, his straight jaw, the veins pulsing at the side of his neck, and the perfect slope of his nose. Adrenaline surges through my veins, my head lightens, and my skin becomes itchy. Something familiar pangs in my chest. It almost feels like déjà vu—like a part of me has lived this moment with this man before.

He doesn't say or move, seeming lost in his thoughts as he gazes down at me.

Birds call in the distance, and I'm knocked out of our trance, pulling back and yanking my arm free from his grasp.

He shakes his head as if gathering his thoughts. "Sorry, you shouldn't go back out into the woods by yourself. It's dangerous, especially now that it's getting dark."

A small voice inside of me yells that this man is dangerous. His story about the chains in his cottage doesn't seem to make sense, and his entire essence screams danger, but if he wanted to murder me, wouldn't he have done it by now?

I know one thing for sure. If anyone knows more about the attacks, it's him. He lives just seconds from where it transpired and appears to be the only park ranger. Although it terrifies me, I need to meet with him again and get some answers.

Leaves crunch as Jack's truck drives down the trail toward where the stranger and I stand.

God, I don't want to deal with Jack again, but it doesn't seem like I have a choice.

I take a deep breath and extend my hand to the stranger. "I'm Red. I'd like to talk to you again."

The stranger gives me a quizzical look before accepting my hand and shaking it with a strong grip. "Okay, Red." He gives me a devilish smirk.

Jack's car door slams. "Red, are you okay?" He rushes toward me, his eyes examining me before turning to the dark stranger whose hand still grasps mine.

"Cameron," Jack grits through his teeth.

He lets go of me. "Jack, what a delight."

They know each other. I'm not sure if this makes things better or worse, but now I have a name for the stranger. Cameron.

9

REHASH THE PAST

"So, how do you know Cameron?" I ask, resting my head against the window of Jack's truck. I should give him the silent treatment after our argument at the diner. I'm still pissed at him, but the journalist inside of me needs answers. Plus, he did rescue me at Granny's request.

Jack and Cameron didn't speak a word to each other. Cameron just grunted his acknowledgment at Jack and returned to his cottage, leaving Jack and me alone by his truck. I got in without another word, and now here we are—just the two of us.

Jack sighs. "It's a long story. I'm more concerned about what happened when you went out to that clearing. Are you sure you're okay?" He scans me. His eyes move frantically as he looks away from the road momentarily.

The rain has started up again, and it's night, making the road before us a hazy black. I wish Jack would continue paying more attention to getting me back to Granny's house in one piece and be less concerned if I have a scraped knee.

I give an aggravated sigh. "Fine, if you refuse to tell me anything, then I'll just ask Cameron."

"No, Red. You can't do that. Cameron is dangerous." His voice has an edge as he grips the steering wheel tighter.

I believe Jack. I figured Cameron was dangerous based on his dominating presence and the fact that he has chains in his house. Just moments ago, I was sure Cameron would chop me up into little bits and eat me for dinner, but from our last moment together and how Jack responds to him, it's clear he's just the person I need to help me solve this case. Sure, he could still dismember me, but it's a risk I'm willing to take if I can discover what's going on in these woods.

Hmm, maybe I am a workaholic.

I sigh. "You mean dangerous, like finding out more about the attacks is dangerous? If that's the case, then sign me up for danger. Cameron just became my new bff."

I scream when Jack jerks the truck off the road and parks in the grass on the side of the road. He turns to me, his eyes an angry blaze. He's so close to me that his giant truck doesn't seem big enough.

"What are you doing?" I yell. Maybe Jack wasn't the right person to come and save me. He's obviously a crazy person.

Jack unbuckles his seatbelt and looms over me, his arms supporting his body weight on the middle console. "Don't you understand I care about you? This isn't just you trying to do a simple job; you aren't just some random girl." He slams his fist against the dashboard. "Fuck, Red. Are we just not going to talk about what happened at graduation? Are we just going to pretend that you weren't the closest thing to me, and then it all disappeared in a moment?"

My head whirls. I knew Jack was just using his proximity to the case to rehash the past. "Why are you doing this to me? Are you trying to hurt me again? I'm here to solve a case, one that I know you know more about. It's painful to be near you. It's painful to think about our last moments together, and it's painful that you seem so interested in me now that I'm not overweight."

We're way off track right now. We should be arguing about why he's refusing to tell me anything more about the attacks and why he seems so set on making me distance myself from anyone connected. But obviously, we will get nowhere if we don't bring up the past. Jack has been holding the case over my head like a carrot, and our last time together is the reason for everything.

Jack's face pinches in disgust. "What are you talking about? Did you hit your head? Our last conversation was when I confessed my love for you, and you rejected me. I have always loved you, and you turned me down and left. I'm the one who should be hurt. Except my feelings never went away. I could never stay mad at you, and I'll do anything to protect you."

He's not lying. He did confess his "love" for me that graduation night, right before the earthquake that set the town in a tizzy, but that was the problem.

The rain pelts against the metal roof, adding to the dramatics and making me raise my voice. "You never loved me. You only told me that because I was leaving and you were staying here. You wanted to fuck with my head. I have loved you ever since we were little kids, and you never thought of me as anything more than your chubby friend. I never went to prom, I never had a first date, I never had anything romantic because I couldn't get over you. I don't care if you thought you might have feelings for me at the moment or not, but you said those things to try to make me stay in this miserable town with you. Not because you actually cared about me."

He slinks back as if I threw a brick at him. "How could you say that? Why would I do something so evil? I was your best friend." His emotions are bubbling over, and the ligaments strain from his neck.

I turn my head away from him, staring out into the rain. "You didn't think I saw you at that party before graduation night, but I did. I overheard you talking to the guys on the football team. They were making fun of me, and you didn't say anything. You just nursed your beer and laughed. How could someone who suddenly loves me the next day think of me as a chubby, silly friend just the night before? You did it to hurt me, to fuck with my head. I've had years to think about it, and I know that's the reason why."

Jack gives a forced laugh and faces the road before him. "That's why you left the party without telling me," he says, mostly to himself.

I don't reply, and a silence passes over us. Maybe this will be the end of it. He can't hide behind his romanticized teenage story he's made up for himself. People are truly who they are when they think no one is looking, and I know who he really is. Maybe now he'll do the right thing, tell me what he knows about the case, and be out of my life for good.

Jack leans back over me. "You know I punched Todd Silvers that night."

"What?" His response catches me off guard. This is the last thing I expected him to say.

He leans in closer, his lips inches away from mine and his eyes dark and focused. "I punched Todd for making fun of you. He was the one who started it, so

I broke his nose. You must have run away right before it happened."

"Oh," I say, my voice shaking. My breath hitches, and the air around me thickens. My brain tries to play catch up. Does this change anything? My body has an immediate reaction, though, not giving a fuck about what my brain thinks.

"I would never let someone talk about you that way." He grabs the back of my neck, and surprisingly, I don't push him away. "I've always loved you, ever since we were kids. I just wanted you to know my true feelings before you left."

My heart beats wildly, and I can't bring my gaze away from his lips.

His eyes study me, and it's like a switch goes off in his brain once he realizes I'm not fighting him. He leans in, capturing my lips with his.

My body ignites into a million flames.

He pulls me closer, one hand on the back of my neck, the other on my shoulders.

He breaks away for a moment, studying my face again.

This time, I lean in, climb over the middle console, and straddle him in the driver's seat.

He brings his lips to my ear, hopelessly out of breath, his scruff rubbing against my sensitive skin. "Red, I've dreamed about this for so long." One of his hands trails down my back, grabbing my ass and grinding me against him. His other hand clutches my breast over my shirt.

I want to say the same. God, how many nights have I dreamed of being wrapped in Jack's arms like this? And that was just when he was a scrawny teenager. Now he's a muscled lumberjack sex god. "Fuck," is all I manage to get out through moans as I throw my head back.

His lips devour mine again as his hand finds the seam of my shirt, trailing up until he gets to my breast. He moves aside my bra and grabs me.

I lean back and pull my shirt and bra over my head before crashing back into him. I buck closer to him, feeling his hardening length through his jeans. I already know it's impressive, and my mouth salivates, thinking about it inside of me.

As one of his hands rubs over my hardened nipples, the other grabs at my ass. "I need you out of these now," he growls in my ear.

He doesn't need to say more. I pull back, fidgeting with the button of my jeans. Why did I decide to wear jeans today? They're still damp from the rain, and I know they'll be a bitch to remove, especially in our tight corridors.

As if by some cruel fate, lights and sirens blare from behind us.

I yelp, jumping off Jack's lap and pulling my tank top back over my head.

When the officer knocks on Jack's window, he's a second too late to see my naked breasts.

"Everything okay, Officer?" Jack asks as he rolls down the window, letting a mist of rain inside the truck. His hair is a tousled mess, and he works on straightening out his shirt.

The raincoated officer shines a flashlight into the truck, I bet, revealing how obviously "about to fuck" we look. My eyes catch my bra on the middle console, and I grab it. *Shit, that wasn't obvious or anything.*

The police officer gives us a smirk. "Just checking to make sure you all were okay. Everything working alright with your truck?"

Jack runs his hand through his hair. "Yes, all good. We just pulled to the side to have a conversation."

The police officer laughs. "Alright, well, be on your way then. It's dangerous to be parked on the side of the road during a night like this."

"Thank you, Officer. We will." Jack rolls his window up as the cop walks away.

I finally breathe out, not realizing until now how long I've been holding my breath. With it comes a forced laugh.

I turn to Jack, and he's laughing, too, as he pulls his truck back onto the desolate road.

Adrenaline still runs through my veins, but the mood has shifted. I'm unsure where Jack and I are heading next or what this all means for us. But I don't have to wonder long because Jack speaks. "Alright, let's get you back to Granny's. You've had a long day."

I nod, but a rock falls to my stomach. It looks like I'll be having more frustrated dreams alone in my bedroom tonight.

10

NOW IT'S PERSONAL

The clanks of pots and pans from downstairs remind me of the thin structure of Granny's walls. Growing up, there was no such thing as sleeping in on a Saturday, and it seems that sentiment rings true even now. I can't tell if it's just how Granny operates in the kitchen or if it's an attempt to wake me up. I suspect the latter.

I groan and roll onto my back, staring up at my popcorn ceiling, catching the evidence of my childhood glow-in-the-dark stars. I barely slept and don't have to look into a mirror to imagine how completely exhausted I appear.

Jack dropped me off at Granny's last night like a perfect gentleman, the asshole. He left me with a soft kiss and a promise that he'd take me to the site of the attacks tomorrow to pick up my car and fill me in on what he knows. I doubt he'll be a hundred percent truthful at first, but it's a start.

I'm not the type of gal to use my body to get what I want, but I have a creeping suspicion that the more I put out with Jack, the more he'll tell me. I must admit the thought of him draped over my body, pumping into me, makes my toes curl, and I guess I get to have my cake and eat it, too.

It's more than just sex, though. My mind's been a whirling mess since his confession last night. Although I've spent years hardening my heart to him, rationalizing why he did what he did in the worst way possible, I can't help but admit his confession of love did something to me. If I do sleep with him, it will be messier than just a fling.

Then there's everything that happened with my near attack of that beast in the woods and Cameron showing up. Could that beast have been the one that killed all those people? If so, why did it run away when Cameron showed up? Maybe what he said is true, and he does chain them up in his little house in the woods. Maybe Cameron's the scariest beast in the woods, and if that's the case, he definitely knows more than he's leading on. Couple that with Jack not wanting me to go near him. I have half a mind to walk back to Cameron's place to find out what he very clearly knows.

"Red, I made pancakes!" Granny yells from downstairs.

I groan and leave bed, grabbing my phone off my bedside table to catch the time. It's only seven a.m. I love Granny, but I need to wrap up this story so I can get the hell out of here. I might die of exhaustion if I stay any longer.

I drag my feet down the rickety stairs. Granny's placing the stack of steamy pancakes in the center of the wooden table as she looks up at me. "Boy, do you look like shit."

"Granny!" I plop in my usual chair, reaching for the pitcher containing the steaming black liquid that will hopefully bring me back to life.

"You must have had a rough night." She winks, and her lips snap into a devilish smirk.

"Granny! Cut me a break," I say in between my embarrassed grin.

Granny settles into her chair and pours herself a glass of orange juice. "I heard you come home late. I'm not sure how you two separated after dinner, but I guess him picking you up went well?" She brings her glass to her lips, and her eyes sparkle. I called her from Cameron's last night. She obviously knows that the dinner plans took a turn, but I bet she's still holding out that something happened between Jack and me. I mean, she's not entirely wrong.

I think for a moment, looking up at the string of imaginary thoughts laid out before me. "Actually, it went horrible."

Granny's face droops. "Oh, no, what happened?"

"Let me see, well, I walked out on Jack at the diner, went to the site of the attacks in a rainstorm, almost got eaten by some wild animal, met this asshole who kind of saved me, lost my keys, went back to the asshole's house to discover his torture chamber, relieved my past with Jack, and got interrogated by the police. Yep. Pretty shitty night if you ask me."

Granny sighs and shakes her head. "So, are you seeing Jack again? You look in need of a good shag!"

"Granny!" I screech. "Is that really what you care about after everything I just said?" I shake my head and stuff my mouth with a forkful of chocolate chip pancakes. The fluffy texture and the smoothness of the chocolate are enough to bring my sour mood a little sweeter, even with Granny's obliviousness.

Granny shrugs. "I've always liked Jack. He comes from a good family, and you two have always been so close."

"You know what happened between us at graduation." Of course, when I came home crying that night, I told Granny everything. The earthquake's magnitude overshadowed the details of my heartbreak, so maybe she forgot.

"Yes, but that was so long ago, and I think you might have got it wrong. You know he's never stopped asking about you since you left?"

"Yes, Granny. You do like to mention that on every phone call." I put down my utensils. "Why do you want me to be with Jack so bad?" I get that she thinks he's attractive; it's plain to anyone with eyes, but is that really enough to have her care so much after all these years?

She sighs. "Isn't it obvious? If you guys were together, you'd be here more. I think he's a good guy, but I miss you, Red." Tears form in the corner of her eyes.

All of my bitterness from my tiredness and Granny's annoying questions melt away. I reach out and grab her frail hand. "Granny, I'm so sorry. I know I should visit more. It's just been crazy ever since I left for college. Now, this job takes so much of my time, but if I finish this story, it could lead to a promotion. That would mean I'd get more time off." I'm bullshitting. I'd never want to take time off, even if I hope otherwise.

Granny puts her hand over mine and shakes her head. "That's nice, dear. I've always wanted you to follow your dreams, but I want you with me. You're all I have since your parents' deaths."

The mention of my parents heavies my nerves. Granny never talks about my parents' murders. Of course, growing up, I had questions. I was a future investigator journalist, so the need to learn more was inherent, but Granny just told me it was a robbery gone bad while I was at school. The person who committed the murders was never convicted because they were later found dead in their home.

I didn't just take Granny's word for it. My middle school years were spent in the school library looking up everything I could about the murders, but I soon realized nothing was left untouched in their case. The man who murdered them was a poor, crazy man who lived in the woods alone. They believe that he died of a bear attack.

Bear attack.

The trail of my thoughts leads me to a part of my memory that I haven't touched in years. What are the odds that an animal attack also killed the person who murdered my parents? I grew up in this town, and it wasn't like animal attacks were common.

"Granny, did you ever think it was odd that an animal killed Mom and Dad's murderer, and then all these people in the clearing were also killed by an animal?"

She sips her coffee, her face morphing blank—her eyes dead. She shakes her head. "Such a tragedy."

It's not an answer. If anything, she's avoiding my question. Growing up, whenever I brought up my parent's death, it was like a flip switch, and Granny became a hollow porcelain doll. Everyone experiences grief differently, and this must be her coping. Maybe things are more connected, and it will make my parent's death make more sense. Maybe finding out about these attacks will bring Granny closure.

I stand, wiping my hands on the flannel napkin. "Well, I better start getting ready. I have another date with Jack soon."

Granny's expression perks. "Oh, goody!"

I head back up to my room to change, my mind racing. Everything seems to grow more mysterious with these attacks: the police not taking it seriously, Jack's avoidance, the beast in the woods, Cameron's presence, and the similarities involving my parents. I don't think I'm here just for work anymore. This story just got a lot more personal.

11

MONSTROUS CHOPS

"Hi," I say shyly as I jump into the passenger seat of Jack's truck. I didn't plan how Jack and I would interact after last night, but now that I'm seeing him, I have no clue how to behave. It's like I'm back in my high school body, feeling a combination of giddiness and nervousness that make me want to vomit.

"Good morning." He smiles at me, his cheeks rosy, and his eyes sparkle. "I got you a coffee." He offers me a cardboard cup.

"Oh, thanks." I take it from him, grateful I have something to fidget with during this drive. I face straight ahead and take a sip, not wanting to get lost in his eyes.

Jack's gaze burns into the side of my cheek, but after a few moments, he returns his attention to his truck and pulls out of Granny's driveway.

"So, how did you sleep?" I don't have to look at him to know he's smirking.

"Fine." I lie. "How about you?"

"Eh. It could have been better. It felt a little lonely."

I smile, still staring straight ahead. "Is that so? Maybe you should get a dog or something."

"Nah, I'd rather have a different type of company." His hand finds its way to my thigh.

My mission this morning was to use my body to get Jack to do what I want, but now that I'm near him, I know that can't be the case. He's not just some random guy in New York. He's my childhood best friend, my childhood love. We'll all end up getting too attached for our own good, including Granny.

I snap my attention to him and brush him off, my cheeks burning. "Jack, listen. I don't know if what happened last night was a good idea." The fire burning in my core begs to differ, but I ignore it.

He nods but doesn't reply.

"I'm glad we talked about everything and cleared the air, but it's just too complicated at this point. I feel it wouldn't be a "no strings attached" type of situation with you and me, and I live in New York. The only reason I'm here is to figure out about these attacks." I hate the words coming from my mouth, and my body begs me to shut up so I can just fuck around and fulfill all my lifelong fantasies, but I'm an adult. I need to act like one. "If you don't want to help me, that's fine. I won't blame you, but I want you to know I will contact Cameron again to get his help."

I don't know if it's my refusal of him or the mention of Cameron, but his brows furrow, and he clenches his jaw. "Red, I told you this is dangerous. Can't you just trust me to stop digging into this?"

"It's obviously not dangerous enough for you to be involved. Can't you tell me what you know so I don't have to run out into the woods by myself and put myself in danger?"

He doesn't reply; he just keeps his eyes fixed on the road.

I want to beg, but what more can I say? He's either going to help me, or he's not. I can't manipulate him into telling me something he doesn't want to. We have too much history for that.

We don't speak again until we reach the clearing and my parked car. It's not until he switches his car into park that he addresses me. "I care about you, Red. I always have, but some things are better for you not to know about."

His words should make me swoon, but I can't stand how small he makes me feel. "You don't think I can handle myself?" I scoff, turning to him with examining eyes.

He watches me, shaking his head softly, his eyes low as if he's sorry for me.

I shake my head. "I don't need protecting." I jump out of the truck and slam the door, heading for the clearing to look for my keys. Maybe it's best we don't muddy up our relationship. I'm too independent for him, and his protection feels a little too suffocating.

"Red, wait!" Jack runs after me, but I'm already through the dense trees.

I turn over my shoulder to yell at him. "I'm tired of you treating me like a child. I don't need anyone to help..."

A low growl stops me in my tracks. I whip my head forward and am met with a pair of glowing, golden eyes looking down at me. The beast stands a foot taller than me and only a hundred yards away. It licks its monstrous chops before howling and charging toward me.

12

SPIRIT OF THE BEAST

I haven't had many opportunities to test my fight-or-flight instincts, but just like the last time I was in these woods, I freeze. I clench my eyes shut and brace myself for the impact and the inevitable tearing of my flesh. The last thing I see is the terrifying beast, impossibly large and completely otherworldly.

It's like time slows, and I can feel the beast getting closer and closer, but I am also aware of Jack charging from behind me. Guilt runs through my veins that I subjected him to this horrible fate as well. Something else runs through me. It's like a fire burning in my chest and a pang at the ends of my fingertips. My heart beats fast as if something's about to explode from me.

A shriek brings me back to my awareness. I open my eyes to find Jack on top of the grey beast, his hands around its throat and a dagger deep in the beast's neck just above his grasp.

I can't believe what I'm witnessing. Jack is overpowering the beast, struggling on its back as he wrings the life out of it.

Now that I'm not paralyzed with fear, I can make out the animal more. It almost looks like a wolf, but at least double the size, with glowing eyes. Jack's a big guy, but he looks like a jockey riding a horse on top of the thing.

The beast snaps at Jack's thigh, but he's too quick. He moves his leg back and tightens his grip even more, his face red and strained.

"Jack!" I yell and charge toward him. I don't think I can possibly help, but I can't just stand here and do nothing.

"Stay back!" he yells, and it's not long before the creature weakens, collapsing to the forest floor.

Jack doesn't let up until the animal's body lay completely still and lifeless. He stands, his shirt ripped to shreds, revealing his broad and muscular chest covered in scratches and blood. His face is speckled where it sprayed out from the creature's stab wound. He looks down at his kill as he wipes his lips with the back of his hand, making the blood smear over his beard.

I guess the blood is from the beast, and the scraps don't appear to be deep, but I'm not sure if he's hurt more. I find my voice. "Are you okay?"

His gaze springs to me, and it's like he's just now realizing I was there to witness this. His eyes don't hold the same boyhood sparkle I'm so used to. There's something primal and monstrous swimming within him. He doesn't say anything; he just clenches his jaw and charges for me.

Instinctually, I tense, preparing for him to attack me as well, but he doesn't. When he reaches me, he grabs me by the waist and pulls me to him, kissing me as if he'll die if he stops.

I taste the power on his lips, mixed with the irony tang of the creature's blood. The urgency in him, as if he wants to conquer me too, makes my core heat.

He grabs my ass, and I wrap my legs around him as he walks me back and presses me against a tree. He removes his lips from mine to lean back and rip my shirt open, snapping buttons onto the forest floor. He reaches for my breasts, grabbing them so roughly that I'm sure he'll leave bruises.

This isn't the gentle boy of my childhood dreams. This is a man with the spirit of the beast he's just slain. He's nothing like I remember.

Through the haze of my arousal, a clear thought bursts into my mind. Jack just killed a monster with his bare hands without hesitation.

I push against Jack's chest, and he pulls back. "Jack, wait."

He searches my face, and it's like a light switches on behind his eyes, the darkness fading and consciousness returning to him. "Are you okay?" he asks, running his hand down my face.

"I'm fine, but I think you have some explaining to do. What in the hell just happened, and what the hell was that animal?"

His features drop, and he nods, lowering me to the floor. "I know. Let's go back to my place, and I'll tell you everything. It's not safe out here."

He'll tell me everything? It seems too good to be true, but I guess after what I just witnessed, there's no point in him denying me his secrets anymore.

He grabs my hand and leads me away from the tree.

I can't help but glance at the creature before leaving. The sight shocks me, not because of the death and carnage but because it looks so different from when I looked at it last. It's like it's decaying already. The body growing smaller, and the hair seems to melt away, making it seem almost scrawny.

Jack's voice whips me back to him. "Look." He bends down to me and holds something out to me. "I found your keys."

13

FAIRIES AND VAMPIRES

It's only a few minutes before we return to Jack's place, but it seems to go by faster because I can't stop my mind from racing. A drop of water splashes on my nose, and I turn my gaze upward to the gray and angry clouds taking up the sky.

"A storm is supposed to be coming through," Jack says as he opens the door to his cabin and motions for me to enter.

It's Washington, what's new? But the wind hollowing through the trees and the darkness rolling in makes me think this storm might be a bit more violent than usual. It seems fitting after everything I just witnessed.

I can't see anything once the wooden door of Jack's shop slams behind us until he flips a switch, and the warm lights slowly flicker to life.

I follow him to the back of the store, to his living space. "Do you ever have customers?" I know it's a stormy day, but I still can't get over how dusty and untouched it looks in here. Not to mention, we're in the middle of the woods.

"No," he says plainly, not looking back and walking briskly.

Obviously, I could have guessed this, but it's odd that he says it so plainly. What's the point of all of this if he doesn't actually sell things? How does he make a living? I hope all these questions and more are answered soon.

He motions for me to enter his living room before shutting and locking the door behind me.

My heart skips a beat. I know Jack won't hurt me. He just saved my life, but there's a terrifying aura to him right now.

"Follow me," he orders as he walks back to his living room and down a dark hall off to the side.

"Where are we going?" I ask. He said that he would explain things to me. Why is he taking me on an spooky tour of his house?

He doesn't answer; just keeps walking until he gets to the last door in the hallway. He pulls out a ring of keys from his pocket and selects an old-looking one before placing it into the keyhole. He holds the door open for me to enter, then shuts and locks it behind me. The darkness of the room swallows me whole. "Jack!" I cry in a pathetic tone. Okay, maybe Jack will hurt me. Why does the thought send heat to my core?

I jump out of my skin when he pulls the cord in the middle of the room, and the space is illuminated by a singular lightbulb dangling overhead. I see his face first, glowing from the light next to him, but his features are still dark and ominous.

"Where are we?" I ask as I whip around, taking in my surroundings. It seems to be a workroom with tools like saws and hammers on workbenches against all the walls, but as I look closer, I realize these aren't just tools; there are guns, knives, and axes. Dark cloaks with hoods, ropes, and chains hang from hooks in the far corners.

"Jack, what the fuck?"

He walks closer to me, and I back up.

"This is where my real work happens," he says.

"What does that mean?"

"I haven't been honest with you, Red. I don't think anyone really has."

I continue backing away from him until I reach the far wall and spread out my arms to grab something. My fingers find a bat, and I swing it in front of me, making Jack back away. "Stop with the ominous shit. Tell me what the fuck is going on." I know trying to bat him away would be futile. I just witnessed him kill a giant wolf, for fuck's sake, but I'm not just going to give up.

He backs away, calming my nerves a bit. His face softens, and he waves his hands in surrender. "Calm down, Red. I'm not going to hurt you." He looks around as if realizing how creepy his "workroom" is for the first time. "I just brought you here because this room is soundproof. No one can hear what I'm about to tell you. Here." He pulls his knife from his pocket and slides it across the floor to me with his foot—the knife he used to kill the wolf. "Take this."

I don't take my eyes off him but scramble to the ground to pick it up.

"I'm just going to grab some chairs for us. I have a lot to explain, so this will take a while." He walks over to a desk in the corner and drags two wooden chairs into the middle of the room, setting them under the singular light.

He sits in the one closest to the door and motions for me to sit next to the other.

When I resist, still clutching the knife, he sighs. "Red, it's me. I'm not going to hurt you. Don't you think I would have had enough opportunities by now if that's my grand plan?"

He's right, of course, and his words do send a sliver of reassurance to my nervous system, but I don't relax completely as I sit in the chair across from him.

He gives me a soft smile, folding his large and bloodied hands on his lap.

It's the first time since the clearing I've noticed the blood all over him. I reach out and grab his hand. "Are you okay?"

He shutters at my touch and looks down. "I'm fine. This isn't any of my blood."

"Right." I pat his hand before pulling back, realizing I also have animal blood all over my hands. I look down the span of my body, realizing that I'm covered in blood, too, due to our steamy embrace. I need a shower, but it'll have to wait because I'm finally about to get answers. In fact, I have a feeling I'm about to get more than I bargained for.

Jack sighs. "Before I tell you anything, you need to promise you won't tell anyone this."

"Jack, I'm a reporter. This is why I'm here. You can't just tell me I can't write about anything."

He leans forward. "Red, this is serious." The fire heats in his eyes again, and my insides quiver. "This is bigger than some story for your job. This is your family history. People's lives are at stake."

"Family history? What are you talking about?" I can't see how any of this has to do with me. Then I think of Granny's weird comments about my parent's death this morning.

"I can't tell you anything until you promise to keep it to yourself. After you learn everything, you'll understand why."

My recorder scorches my leg inside my pocket. I'll probably regret this promise later, but what more can I do? I need to know, and now it seems more personal than ever. "Okay, fine. I promise I won't tell."

Jack studies my face for a moment before nodding. He brings his hand to the back of his neck and rubs at it as he rolls his head back and forth. "Well, first, let's talk about what just happened in the woods."

"Yes, let's." I lean forward.

"Do you know what that animal was?"

"Some mutated wolf or something? Is that what killed all those people?"

"Not necessarily just a mutated wolf. It's a were-wolf, and yes, a few of them killed all those people."

"Werewolf?" I sit back, studying Jack, unsure if he's joking or deranged. "You mean like from fairytales?"

He rolls his eyes. "Sort of like the ones from fairy-tales, except these are real. They change from humans to monsters."

I can't help the laugh that escapes from me. "Jack, werewolves aren't real."

He leans forward, his expression growing more in-tense. "Red, yes they are."

My tone tightens. "Are you fucking with me? Are you still trying to get out of telling me the truth by telling me something ridiculous?"

"Red, you came here because the attacks were suspicious. You knew that there was something different about these animal attacks. What were you expecting to discover?"

I get up from my seat, treading to stop the energy bubbling inside me from bursting. "I don't know, maybe some sick bastard using animals as weapons or a murderer staging these kills as animal attacks. I sure as hell didn't come here to learn that fairies and vampires exist."

He sighs. "That's ridiculous. Everyone knows fairies don't live in this part of the world."

I stop and glare at him, my heart pounding in my head.

He just smiles.

"That's it. If you're going to fuck with me, I'm leaving." I charge toward the locked door, but Jack jumps from his seat and blocks me.

"Wait, Red, stop. Listen, I'm not fucking with you. Werewolves are real. I know it sounds crazy, but you saw that thing in the forest. You know that wasn't just a big, bad wolf."

He's so close to me. I look up at him and try to read his expression.

He places his hand just above my breast, over my heart. "This is part of your blood. I know you can feel it's true."

His touch sends shivers down my skin, but his words ring through my consciousness. "What do you mean it's part of my blood?"

"I'll show you." He walks toward a shelf and reaches for a book, blowing off a layer of dust before bringing it to me. "Look, this is my family history." I grab the book from him and sit in the chair closest to me.

It's a photo album filled with black and white photos and newspaper clippings. It seems organized by time, beginning with older-looking pictures and articles from the early nineteen hundreds.

"Ten Slain in Strange Animal Attack."

"Keep Out of the Woods."

"Another Mysterious Animal Attack."

All the headlines hold a similar theme.

The pictures show groups of men, all wearing matching black capes with axes raised over their shoulders. As time passes, the groups contain a sprinkle of women as well.

"Who are these people?" I ask.

"My ancestors. I come from a long line of Werewolf Hunters."

"Werewolf Hunters? So that's your real job. You hunt werewolves?" I don't know why this seems even more unbelievable than werewolves existing. Who's funding this shit?

"Yes. Look." He flips through the book until he's almost toward the end. He points to a faded picture of a tall and muscular man, his hand on the shoulder of a small red-headed boy. The pair wear matching capes with axes at their sides. "That's me and my dad. That was the day of my first kill. He was so proud of me."

I gaze up at him to catch the longing look in his eyes.

I'm still not sure if this album proves anything. They could just be weird cult members killing wolves and telling themselves they're defeating evil magic. But one thing's for certain, Jack isn't fucking with me. He truly believes what he's telling me.

I glance back at the photo album, flipping to the last page. Out of everything I witnessed tonight, I didn't think there would be anything to shock me anymore, but the moment I see the picture, my heart stops. I run my finger over the faded picture of the blonde woman wearing a cape and leaning against an axe.

"It's my mom."

14

THE STORM

"That's my mom." I don't take my eyes off the picture, and a ringing blares throughout my head. I don't have many pictures of my mom, and she hasn't been alive for so long. Sometimes, she visits me in my dreams, but even that version of her blurs compared to the actual image in my lap. She's young here, maybe nineteen or twenty.

"Your family comes from a long line of Werewolf Hunters, too."

A horrible thought pops into my head. I shoot my gaze to his face and study his features. "Are we related?" My stomach turns sour at the thought. Although we never went very far, it was definitely too close for relatives. We both have the same crimson hair, even if his is more rich than mine, but plenty of people have red hair, right?

"No!" Jack says urgently.

My stomach settles.

"Our families come from very different lines. Your mother's grandparents moved here from Ireland since we have such a large population of werewolves."

The tug of war on my emotions tires me more than I thought possible. I'm unsure if I believe any of this, even if I saw that beast with my own eyes and my mother stares back at me in the "Werewolf Hunter" uniform.

An alarm goes off in my conscious, pieces of the puzzle falling together. I shoot to my feet, the photo album still clasped in my hand. "Jack, does this have to do with my parents' murders?"

He suddenly looks tired and walks toward me. He directs me back into one of the chairs and pulls the other close to mine before sitting. Our knees touch as he takes my hands.

He's quiet for a moment as if gathering the words. "Not all of your blood is of Werewolf Hunters."

"What does that mean?"

"Your father, he was half werewolf."

I almost want to punch him. I know he truly believes what he's telling me, but for him to say that my dead father is some mystical make-believe character makes me sick. "Jack," I say, pulling back. All of this is too much.

He holds my hands tighter. "Red, I know this is hard to hear and even harder to believe, but listen. Your mother fell in love with him even though the hunters urged her not to. The two went above all suggestions. Even Granny was against it, but then you came, and she softened."

"Granny? She knows about this?" If I could have one other person confirm or deny things, maybe this would start to make sense.

He holds my gaze, but I can't help but notice a slight dart in his eyes. "She used to. She was attacked, trying to avenge your parents. She doesn't remember most things. Sometimes, I see her memory of her heritage return in flashes, but it's rare and short-lived."

I think about the look in Granny's eyes this morning. Is this why she always short-circuits whenever I bring up my parents?

"Who killed my parents then?"

"The werewolves. They were even more unhappy about your father being with a Hunter. They feared that if your parents were to have a son, it could be powerful and that it could be swayed to use its powers to kill werewolves."

I knew the murder of my parents seemed suspicious, even from a young age. But this... This is just all too much.

"How do you know that? How do you know what the werewolves wanted?"

"My father killed the werewolf that killed your parents. He tortured him until he got the truth. My parents were both killed by werewolves—my mother when I was just a child and then my father just a few years ago. I'm the leader of the Hunters now. Even though my father and I never had the best relationship, I'll do anything to avenge my parents. I know you can relate."

My heart aches for Jack, and I bring my hand to his face, sensing the sadness in his eyes. He believes this.

I'm unsure if I believe this myself, but this is a source of pain for Jack, and I must hear him out.

I look around the room at the weapons and tools, wondering if torture is used often. It sure seems like they have the equipment to do so. Even with everything Jack tells me, I can't bring myself to hate a whole group of—people, creatures, whatever they are. "But all werewolves can't be bad. Do you kill all of them? Even someone like my father?"

He sighs, looking down at my hands and rubbing his callused fingers over my palms. "There's only one family of werewolves we're unable to kill. It's the only one with a public identity—the rest we must hunt out of hiding. Red, your dad seemed like a good man, but that's because he was half-human. Werewolves eat humans. It's hard to say that any of them are good when it's in their nature to destroy us."

I pull back. "I don't like that sentiment."

He doesn't let me go. "They killed our parents without any mercy. They were going to kill you if you developed any powers. Thankfully, you never showed any sign. They've been watching you, ensuring you haven't grown into them, and now you want to write a story about their attacks. You couldn't put a bigger target on your back."

Maybe it wasn't just a coincidence that werewolves found me in the clearing both times I was there. Maybe they're hunting me.

I lean back in my chair, letting my head fall back. "I don't know, Jack. This is all too much. I don't even know if I believe it."

He sighs. "I know."

I wrack my brain for a way he can prove this to me. Suddenly, an idea pops into my consciousness. "What about that werewolf you killed in the clearing? Will it change back to a human now that it's dead?" I picture its lifeless body, looking smaller as we walked away.

Jack sits up straight, excitement in his eyes. "Yes, I can show you."

A crack shakes the wooden walls around us. Rain patters against the roof as if it's bullets.

Jack gets up from his chair and charges toward the door, unlocking it and walking down the hallway. I follow him until he reaches the window in his living room. Sheets of rain fall from the sky, making it impossible to see anything outside. It's only mid-day, but it might as well be the middle of the night. As if on cue, the lights give out, enveloping us in total darkness.

Jack goes to the kitchen and rummages around his cabinets, pulling out three candles and lighting them. He sighs and pulls out his phone. "It looks like this storm isn't letting up. It's supposed to be like this until tomorrow morning. You should probably call Granny and make sure she's okay."

He hands me his phone, but the line rings dead. "She can't pick up calls from her landline if she lost power too."

He nods. "Well, it looks like you might be spending the night if it doesn't let up at all."

"Uh."

"If you have to sleep here, I'll take the couch, and you can have the bed." My expression must be obvious even in the dim light of the candles. He looks hurt.

I feel bad and want to reassure him that it's not that I don't want to sleep with him. Even after everything that happened today, god, do I still want to fuck him, but that's the problem. I don't even know if he's crazy or not. We have too much history, and now we're bringing in our literal family history mixed with werewolves and goblins. It's too much for us to try anything.

"I have a generator. I'll turn it on so you can shower and clean up."

I look down at my blood-smeared and tattered clothes. "Right, thanks."

Jack walks back into his shop, leaving me alone with my thoughts.

My blood feels heavy as I stare out the window. I've grown up in Dayton my whole life. I know the storm isn't clearing up anytime soon. I'm staying the night with a Werewolf Hunter.

15

ONE NIGHT

I step out of the shower to find one of Jack's green flannels and a pair of his boxers laid out for me on the bed. I crack open his door. "Can I wear these?"

"Yeah," he calls from the kitchen. "Sorry, it's all I have."

"It'll work. Thanks." I shut the door and let my towel fall to the floor before pulling on Jack's clothes. I'm enveloped in his musky smell, and I can't stop myself from bringing the collar of his shirt to my nose and breathing him in.

It takes a second for me to realize what I'm doing. No, I can't be sniffing his clothes and reveling in how they feel on my skin. If I have any chance of surviving this night without digging Jack and I's confusing relationship into an even bigger hole, I must keep my hormones in check.

His flannel swallows me, the bottom landing at the top of my thighs. Thank God he brought me some of his boxers, or he would definitely see everything if I bent over. I can't help thinking about his naked body wearing these clothes as I pull the boxers over my ass. God, I need to get it together.

When I've finally dressed, combed my fingers through my wet hair, and taken a few deep breaths, I step out of Jack's bedroom.

He's in the kitchen, cooking something on the stovetop.

"What are you making?" I ask as I slide into one of the bar stools facing the kitchen.

"Spaghetti." He turns away from the stove to catch my eyes. He freezes, his eyes wide and his Adam's apple bobbing. You'd think I'd stepped out wearing a ballgown instead of his hand-me-downs. His eyes soak me in as if they're dying of thirst.

My cheeks heat, and I look down at my hands, unable to take the attention for much longer before sitting on his couch.

He clears his throat. "Do those work?" he asks, walking over to me with a plate full of spaghetti and placing it on the coffee table in front of me.

I turn my attention back to him. "Yep. Thanks." His hair is wet, making his red hair look brown, and he's wearing a white T-shirt and grey sweatpants. God, grey sweatpants? It's like he's trying to seduce me.

"You were able to shower?"

"Yeah, I have another shower at the back of the shop. It's for when I get too dirty for my own shower. I changed in the bedroom while you were showering."

My mind races with images of him naked in his bedroom with me just on the other side of the door, sopping wet. If only I took a shorter shower and stumbled in on him. I shake my head slightly, trying to rid my mind of my dirty thoughts. God, I hope this storm stops. I don't think I'll be able to take much more of this.

But the storm doesn't stop. In fact, it gets worse. The winds howl, shaking the glasses in the cabinets, and the rain sounds like a constant pour of water from above. I've never been scared about a little thunderstorm, but this seems more than that. I can't help but wonder if the dead werewolf just a few hundred feet away from Jack's cabin could have something to do with it. It's illogical, but so are werewolves in general.

"Are you sure we're safe here?" I ask, pulling my knees closer to my chest on his grey couch.

Jack leans over in front of me to pick up my empty plate of spaghetti. Not only is he hot, he's a damned good cook. Who knew something as simple as spaghetti could taste so good? I probably looked like an animal, scarfing down everything on my plate.

"We're safe. I promise. It's just a rough storm. These windows are hurricane-proof."

Even in my fright, I can't help but notice the buzz of electricity that bounces off him when he's so near. My heartbeat increases, and I have to close my eyes to focus on anything else than how damned good he looks in his fucking stupid grey sweatpants.

"Are you getting sleepy?" he asks from the kitchen sink as he washes our dishes.

My eyes pop open, and I turn to him. "What time is it?"

He turns to look at a clock on the wall behind him. "It's eight."

Figures. I'm not even a little tired, especially with the adrenaline pumping through my veins after everything that's happened today, but maybe going to bed is the best idea. We need space between us, and maybe his bedroom door would be enough.

I give a fake yawn, throwing my hands over my head. "Yeah, I think today just wore me out." I stand. "Are you sure you're okay with me taking your bedroom?"

He abandons the dishes, wipes his hands on his pants, and walks toward me. "Of course. Is there anything you need? Are you warm enough?" It's like he's a mother hen clucking over me. It's so odd that just hours ago, I watched him kill a wild beast—a werewolf—with his bare hands and felt terror deep in my veins when he locked me in his torture chamber, and now he's making me spaghetti and ready to tuck me into a warm bed.

I shake my head. I don't have the strength to perform a psychoanalysis on Jack. "I'm fine. I'm just going to call it a night." I turn toward his bedroom, moving a little faster than normal, shutting the door and resting against it before closing my eyes.

It's just one night. I need to keep it in my pants, and then I can figure everything out tomorrow.

***

The rain pelts against the window, and I curl deeper into Jack's thick comforter. His bed smells like him, and I bring a corner of the blanket up to my nose, finding that the smell washes me with a sense of comfort: comfort and so much more.

Why did I think sleeping in his bed before I was tired would be a good idea? Sure, I don't have to be near him anymore, but now my mind can't stop racing with images of him sleeping here—wishing he was here with me.

I toss to my other side for the twelfth time, trying to count sheep or think about some boring email I need to send to my boss in the morning, but it doesn't help. My body vibrates with adrenaline, and sleep seems so far down shore that I'll never be able to reach it.

I sit up, looking around his dark room, trying to find something to distract me from the feelings swirling through my veins. My eyes adjust to the darkness, and lightning reveals more of the room every few minutes.

His dresser sits bare, and he doesn't even have a sock lying in the corner. His room is meticulous, so there's nothing to distract me.

I lean over and grab my phone off the nightstand. Of course, it's dead. I sigh and grab the covers, noticing a top sheet neatly tucked into the mattress. I stick my legs into the opening, but once I'm underneath, I realize it's entirely too snug, and I'm like a trapped bug.

I kick my arms and legs, but it's no use. I crawl out from the comforter and lean over the side of the bed, pulling at the sheets. Did he superglue his bed together? How is this so difficult? Thunder roars into the room, and something smacks against the window. I scream and fall out of bed.

His footsteps slam down the hallway, and the bedroom door bursts open. "Red, are you okay?"

I'm thankful it's dark because my cheeks burn as I pick myself off his floor and struggle to my feet. "Yes, sorry, I just fell out of bed." I rub at my sore elbow as my eyes catch his shirtless figure stepping closer to me. My throat clogs, and I take a step backward, clenching the damn top sheet behind me. "I, uh, it's these sheets. I tried to get under them, but they're so tight."

"Oh." He runs his hand through his messy hair, eyes searching my body. "Sorry, my dad always made sure my bed was military-grade, and I guess it's just a habit that stuck. Here, let me help you." He's so close to me, and he reaches down to pull the sheet out from the bottom of the mattress.

"No, it's okay. You should get back to bed." I can't take being so near to him. The words jumble out of my mouth as if they're a rushing faucet. I try to push him away, but when my hands touch his arms, I realize it's a mistake.

His skin is warm, and his earthy scent seems to wrap around me and pull me closer. I close my eyes, pressing my body against his as he turns toward me and wraps me in his arms.

His body is hard against mine, and before I can talk myself out of it, I reach up and wrap my arms around his neck, pulling his lips to mine.

It's like the flick of a switch: the energy in the room shifts, and my brain flashes blank—my want completely takes over, and the need to have him draped over every inch of me consumes me. His hands move quickly. He grabs my ass, pulling me against him as I wrap my legs around his waist.

He breaks away from our kiss, and his lips find my ear. "Red," he whispers. "Oh, God." He leans me back against his bed, his body never leaving mine. I taste the desperation on his tongue as it pushes deeper into me. The years of pent-up want taste so good, and it's like he's consuming me from the inside out.

I reach for the bottom of my shirt, wanting—needing, to feel his bare skin against mine. Before I even get it over my belly button, Jack's hands push mine away, and he's yanking it off me, nearly tearing it in half.

The moment we separate for the shirt to be pulled over my head is too much. It's like my cells are holding their breath and can barely take the lack of contact. Jack's nerves must feel the same way, too, because he swoops down, one hand gripping my breast and the other wrapped around the back of my throat. His touch isn't gentle; it's as if he's tortured, and my body is his only source of reprieve from his pain.

My feet work down his sweatpants, and I reach to feel him. "Oh, my god." I pull away to moan, and he shutters as my hand wraps around his length. Jack's a big guy. I never doubted that he'd be packing, but as

I slowly stroke up and down, I can barely believe how large and thick he is.

"Red, slow down," he whispers into my ear with a rush of forced air.

I'm already moving as slowly as possible, but my simple touch seems too much for him. A fire drops to the pit of my stomach at the thought of how much he wants me. This moment is all of my horny teenage dreams come true. The power that zips through my veins that he wants me as much—maybe even more than I want him, is almost too much.

He pulls away from me, grabs the boxers I'm wearing, and pulls them down my legs. Once I'm completely bare, he holds himself up with his arms, his eyes moving up and down my body. He turns his head away from me and bites his lips. "Fuck, Red. I can't believe this is finally happening."

I'm thinking the same thing, but I don't want to think. If I think, I'll talk myself out of this. Even though every cell of my body has melted and the urge to have him inside me is one I don't think I could quelch on my own, there's a part of my brain that knows this is a bad idea.

I reach up and grab his neck, pulling him back into me. "Fuck me," I whisper into his ear, grabbing his cock and positioning it at my entrance.

He resists for a second as if he wants to take his time. I'm sure the man could ravish me in a hundred possible ways, but right now, I don't have time for it. This is years of pent-up sexual frustration, and I need him inside of me urgently. I wiggle my hips under him, grinding against him, and finally, he snaps. He jerks up, slamming open his bedside drawer and grabbing a condom. He rips it open with his teeth and hurriedly rolls it on. He crashes his lips into mine and pushes himself into me. It all happens so fast; I'm thankful he has a brain cell left to make the smart call. I cry out at his first thrust, the size of him causing pain to shoot up my body.

"Are you okay?" He pulls back, studying me.

I nod. "Keep going," I beg.

He kisses down my neck and slowly pulls out and back in. The pain lessens with each thrust, and within a matter of seconds, I'm swirling into an abyss of pleasure. His abs rub against my clit as he works himself deeper and deeper with each thrust.

"This is too good," he moans. "Fuck, Red. This is too good."

His encouraging words bring me close to that edge, my nails digging into his back as his speed increases until he pulses inside of me—filling me. He moans into my ear, and my whole body shutters as the wave of my orgasm rushes over me. It's overpowering, flattening me and tearing me in half. The rush lasts longer than I've experienced before, and I cling to Jack until I reach the shore, my body relaxing under his.

Jack peppers kisses down my neck and over my breast, and I shutter, my skin suddenly sensitive. He lies next to me, nuzzling into the crook of my neck, his breath slow and heavy.

I lie still, the damn top sheet tangled around my legs, but the rest of me bare. Now that my body is back to its neutral state, I realize what we've done.

Jack's chest rises and falls against me, and in a few short moments, I can tell he's drifted off to sleep. No thoughts of the future or what this means swirl around his mind.

As for me, I can't stop thinking. This wasn't just a simple fuck. This is Jack. My Jack. And now there's the whole supernatural that's come into play. Although my body feels better than it has in a long time, my brain feels the opposite. I'm fucked—in all ways possible.

16

MYSTERY OF LIFE

S leeping through one of the worst storms to hit Dayton was bad enough. Trying to do so next to a naked beefy lumberjack of my childhood dreams made sleep a mythical treasure I couldn't capture.

Sure, my body had a short-lived reprieve from the insistent need that turned my nerves to angry crickets ever since I laid eyes on Jack, but it didn't last long. With his muscular arms clenching my side, his chest taking in steady breaths, and his deep and familiar smell swirling around me throughout the night, it took everything in me not to wake him up and go for round two.

On the other hand, Jack slept like a log, which irritated me beyond end. How can his brain not be jumbled with what this all means? I live in New York. He lives here. We can't have a relationship, and after the night we had, I don't know how I will forget about him and move on.

As the morning sun shines into the cracks of the windows, it's like the faucet of some heavenly sink shuts off. Birds chirp in the distance, and it feels as if Mother Nature is finally happy now that I've given in to my urges.

I slowly remove Jack's arm from my waist and pull myself out of bed. I find my jeans in the corner of the room, still covered in mud and blood, and pull them over Jack's boxers. I'm already mortified to walk into Granny's home in such a state, but this is all I got.

I step out into the living room, my eyes catching my keys on his countertop. Before I can even make it to the door, Jack's voice meets my eardrums. "Where are you going?"

I twirl around, my heart hammering out of my chest like a burglar caught in the act. His grey sweatpants are back over his tree trunk legs, and he's buttoning his flannel over his boulder of a chest. "Are you trying to sneak out of here?"

"Uh." I search his living room as if something will catch my eye and give me an excuse. I sigh once an inappropriate amount of time has passed, and I've come up blank. "I should get back home to Granny. I'm worried about her."

Jack walks closer to me. "Okay, well, you don't need to sneak out of here like I'm some guy you just met last night." My nerves tighten at his words, but his expression remains calm as he walks closer to me, pulling me into his arms once he reaches me.

Oh God, this is bad. He's in love, and I don't think that's something I know how to deflect. Most of my life was spent loving Jack. My adult world can't handle the messiness that comes from this.

"It's okay, Red." He smiles down at me.

My eyes snap to meet his. "What's okay?"

"I can tell you're freaking out."

"What? I'm not freaking out." I break my stare, my eyes darting as if they're a cat chasing after a laser beam.

He laughs. "We had sex last night, and it was great." He leans down, his lips hovering over my ear. His hot breath sends shivers down my spine. "And hopefully we can do it again." He pulls me against him, and I feel his hardened length through his sweatpants. "The sooner the better."

A quiet moan escapes me, and I shut my eyes to clear my head.

Jack pulls me back. "But I know that you live in New York, and I live here. I'm not trying to sink my teeth into you and make you stay." He pulls me back and kisses down my neck, his teeth grazing my skin. "Well, maybe I do want the teeth part."

I gasp, my nerves alight, and clench his biceps as if I'll turn into a puddle without him pressed up against me.

He reaches my lips, softly teasing me with his, but then pulls away.

My eyes shoot up, and I look at him as he clenches his lips. "You're right, though. You should get back to

Granny's." He steps back, running his hand through his hair. "And I've also got a mess to clean up."

Reality crashes around me. I almost forgot about the "werewolf" Jack killed last night and the rest of the revelation that came after. There's still so much to figure out besides Jack and I's relationship. It seems my entire heritage is a mystery, and seeing this werewolf body is only the first step in uncovering my past.

"I'll walk you to your car." He looks down, and his cheeks redden. "Maybe I should change my pants first."

My eyes follow down from his open flannel, revealing his muscular chest, to the grey sweatpants that hide absolutely nothing. Although he says we must stay focused and deal with everything from last night, his body betrays him.

My cheeks heat, and I can't hide the smile forming at the corner of my lips.

He smiles but shakes his head before turning to his bedroom.

***

The mood shifts the moment we walk out from Jack's place to the woods. The quiet of the early morning wraps around me and perks all my senses to attention. The smell of the wet foliage makes everything seem fresh and new, but it doesn't mask the doom swirling around us as we walk to the clearing.

Jack and I don't say a word. For me, it's mostly out of fear. I don't want to summon another werewolf attack. Jack's never been much of a talker, and I hope he's not as terrified as I feel. One of us needs to be strong.

Jack walks a few steps ahead of me, entering the clearing before I do. "Shit."

"What?" I jog to remove the space. I'm not sure why I'm hurrying to see whatever has upset the Werewolf Hunter, but the curiosity of my journalistic brain can't help but be eager to discover. I step next to Jack, scanning the empty field around me. It hits me—the field is empty. There's no dead monster. There's no dead man. The body is gone. The only evidence that it was here is broken branches and small traces of blood smeared on the ground.

"Where did it go?" I ask. I search the side of Jack's face. This body was supposed to confirm everything

Jack told me last night. Could he have gone out in the middle of the night and moved it so he could keep messing with me? No. That's even crazier than this all being real, but my rational part can't ignore the idea.

"His pack must have moved it. That would explain the storm last night." He kicks at the ground and walks over to the spot where the body lay yesterday.

"Werewolves can cause storms?" I can't say it didn't cross my mind, but it seems so unbelievable.

"Some. They have all types of fucked up powers, and they become even more powerful once they find their mates."

"Mates? Like their partners?"

"It's an invisible bond between two werewolves. They're destined for each other whether they like it or not. Some werewolves don't ever find their mate, which makes it easier for us, but the ones that do... they are even more dangerous."

He squats to analyze the ground. "This isn't good. Werewolves are vengeful creatures. They're going to come after us."

"Us? I didn't kill it."

"Yeah, but he was tracking you, and now he's dead. They know a Werewolf Hunter killed him and that you are part Werewolf Hunter. They've always viewed you as a threat, and now they have something to pin on you."

"Well, that's great."

He stands, rushing toward me. "You got to get out of here. Get back home to Granny, and I'll take care of this." He presses against the small of my back and leads me out of the clearing to my car.

I don't say anything—my brain jumbles. I still don't have proof that werewolves exist. Sure, I trust Jack, but the reporter in me can't just take things for face value. I need proof. I need undeniable evidence. It's always been my mission when reporting on a story, but I need this more than ever.

This isn't just a story anymore. This is the mystery of my life.

17

DARK AND DANGEROUS MAN

Thank God I have an extra pair of clothes in my car. My hands shake as I pull on a fresh pair of jeans and strategically switch my t-shirt to an old concert shirt from a few years ago. I glance at the clock on my dashboard. It's not even eight in the morning. The road is desolate, so I don't worry about anyone getting a free show as I change.

I pull down the visor and run my hands through my hair, examining the damage. Surprisingly, I don't look too bad. A shower and a fuck did me good, but even with my improved appearance, there's no way I can go back to Granny's. What am I supposed to say to her? "Hey, Granny, are you and my parents part of some mythical werewolf and hunter lore?" If what Jack said is true, she probably won't remember anything. From my experience bringing up my parents to her, I expect the same glaze to wash over her face and her mind to reset.

I plug my phone into my car charger and drive, planning to clear my head anywhere open this early before giving her a call.

It doesn't take long for the park to come into view. Cars pack the parking lot, and soccer games are in full swing on the fields. Perfect. I don't want to be alone right now. I want to be with normal people, living normal lives that have nothing to do with monsters and fairytales. Plus, there's a coffee stand in the center of the park. What could be more perfect?

I pull in, parking in the farthest spot, and walk over to the stand to grab a black coffee. Kids yell all around me, and I catch the tired expressions of their parents as they do their best to wield their children to their next activity. God, I can't imagine exuding so much energy so early in the morning, but right now, being exhausted from dealing with normal children seems much better than being exhausted from werewolf hunting. How did my parents do it?

I walk the edge of one of the fields closest to me, trying to remember everything about my parents as I can. They used to take me to this park. It looked completely different eighteen years ago, but the same large oak trees shaded the park's corners. I remember swinging from them, my dad climbing up after me, pretending that if he caught me, he'd gobble me up. Tears push at the corner of my eye ducts, and I clench my palms, trying to gather my emotions.

I've tried my best not to think about my parents much since their death. It's always been too painful, and once it starts, it leads to a spiral of despair, but now it seems I *need* to think about them—to remember every detail I can to detangle this mess. Sure, I could just go back to New York and put this part of my life behind me, but I'm already in too deep. How can I expect to carry on with all the questions swirling through me?

"Watch out!" someone yells before something bangs against my head.

I fall to the grass, my vision blurry.

"Oh, shit," a gruff voice whispers angrily as the source gets closer. "Are you okay?"

I sit up, my head still swirling but starting to slow. "Yeah, I'm fine," I say, resting my head in my hands to regain my focus. Obviously, I don't feel great, but I'm too embarrassed that I just fell on my ass, and now people are probably staring at me. I need to pretend to be fine and get to my car and cry.

Someone crouches in front of me, and I meet their gaze.

"Shit," he says.

It's like ice water pours down my back. I know that voice.

"Shit," I say back, his face finally steadying before me, his pupils dilating and sucking me in like black holes. His eyes are lighter than before. Maybe it's just because we're out in the sun instead of the dark and rainy forest, but I swear they look as if they hold a glow.

A smile creeps up at the corner of his lips, and he shakes his head before grabbing the soccer ball beside me, standing, and offering me his hand. "Of course, it's you." His dark hair is slicked back, and a small strand falls in the middle of his forehead.

"Of course, it's *you.*" I scowl at him and grab his hand, ignoring the static electricity that jolts through me and lugging myself up.

"Are you just going to repeat everything I say now?" He steps closer, his fingers grazing across the throbbing spot on my head where the ball landed. "Maybe you got hit harder than I thought."

I'm frozen for a moment, his warm touch seeping into my pores, but then I jerk back and swat his hand away.

"I'm fine." I look down, straightening my shirt and wiping leaves from my backside. Seeing Cameron in his dry-fit grey shirt and athletic shorts sobers me from the pain in my head. He's just as handsome as I remembered, even in these dorky camp counselor clothes. "Why did you throw a soccer ball at me?" I ask, looking around the field. Next to me, a co-ed team of kids have their eyes glued to us.

He laughs and throws the ball to the group of children, bringing a silver whistle to his lips and blows. A boy runs up to the ball and kicks it to the group.

All eyes turn away from us and back to the children running around the green field.

"I didn't throw a soccer ball at you. One of the kids just gained superhuman strength and kicked it over here instead of into the net."

My eyes trail up and down his body. "Is one of them your kid?" I can't imagine this dark and dangerous man fathering a child, but seeing him in these more casual clothes, the image starts to materialize in my mind.

He laughs again. "God, no. I'm just a volunteer coach."

"Why?"

He scrunched his face. "Why? Why not?"

I shake my head. Of course, that was a stupid question. The ball may have done more damage to my frontal lobe than I thought. "Sorry, you just don't seem the type of guy to volunteer to coach soccer out of the kindness of your heart." Yep, didn't make it any better.

He arches his neck back. "Shit, you really think poorly of me from our short meeting. May I remind you that I'm a park ranger? Coaching a community soccer team is exactly the kind of activity someone like me would do in my spare time."

I shake my head. "Right. I'm sorry. I've just had a confusing day and am not feeling myself."

The crowd watching the soccer game next to us erupts in boisterous cheers.

We turn our attention to the kids crowding around one child pumping his fists in the air. The goalie of the opposite team swoops up the ball from the net.

Cameron smiles, his dark eyes crinkling as he watches.

The edges of my heart start to melt watching him.

He turns back to me, and I steel my expression, feeling caught. He looks down at my empty paper coffee cup on the ground before leaning to pick it up. "Looks like I owe you a coffee. Stay for a few minutes, and I'll take you somewhere with a decent drip."

"Uhhh..." but before I can answer, he runs back to the field, turning to wink at me before he joins the celebrating team.

It looks like I can't really say no. I should get back to Granny and start figuring out this mess, but then an idea pops into my mind. Cameron is a park ranger who seems to have a history with Jack. If anyone knows about the magical woods, it's him.

18

DEVILISH SMILE

"**I**'m sorry, Granny. I promise my phone just came back to life." I rest my elbow against my car door as I stare outside my window, looking at the log cabin coffee shop Cameron insisted we meet at. Technically, I could have called Granny after plugging my phone in and before wandering around the park, but I needed to clear my head first.

"I promise I'm fine. I told you, I got stuck at Jack's house when the storm blew through, and the power went out, so I couldn't call."

Granny clucks her disapproving worries in my ear, and I hold the phone away, rolling my eyes.

"I know, I know. I love you. I'll be home in a few hours, and we can talk more. Okay, love you, bu-bye."

She's still grumbling as I hang up.

I sigh, feeling shitty. Of course, Granny's worried about me. I'm here to investigate mysterious attacks and then go radio silence for over twenty-four hours. If I were my granddaughter, I'd be notifying the FBI, but Granny isn't a normal Granny. Well, that may or may not be true. I can't help the sliver of doubt nagging at the back of my head that Jack has gone completely nuts and made up an entire werewolf tale to get in my pants. Yeah, that would be a weird plan, but hey, it kind of worked.

Cameron has to know more than he's letting on. If just one more person can confirm what he's saying, maybe I'll completely believe it and discover my past.

Before I leave my car and head inside, I pull up my email on my phone and type a message to Angela, letting her know there's a family emergency that I'll be handling for the next few weeks. After our last phone call, it didn't sound like taking time off would be an issue. Normally, I'd put everything aside to focus on my work, but this is too big, and I know it will take a while to sort through. Even if Jack is crazy, I still need some time to figure shit out.

I sigh before opening my door and exiting my car to head inside.

Walking through the doorway, I immediately catch Cameron sitting at the booth near the back. He waves at me, a steaming cup of coffee cupped in one hand and a matching one across from him.

He exits the booth as I approach, a smile etched on his perfect face. "I was starting to worry that you swerved off the road from a brain injury."

"What?" I give him a disgusted look before sliding into the booth.

His smile fades, and he sits across from me, wrapping his large hands around the white mug. "Remember the soccer ball that just hit your head? Are you sure you're okay?"

As soon as he mentions it, the throb returns slightly. "Oh, yeah. I'm sorry. It's been a day already, and I had to call my Granny and message my work."

He nods. "You mentioned you've been having some rough days." He looks down at the coffee in front of me. "I got you a black coffee, but we can get some cream and sugar if you want." His eyes search the diner as if looking for a waitress to summon.

"No, it's fine. Black is great." I bring the coffee to my lips, taking a tiny sip. Well, shit. He was right. This coffee is good. I don't feel like paying him the compliment for his suggestion, though. I'd rather get to the point.

"So," he says before I can get out my first question. "What did you want to meet with me about?"

I arch my neck back in confusion. "Meet with you? You invited me to coffee." How could he possibly know that I had ulterior motives for meeting him?

He sighs and shakes his head. "Remember when we met? Before you left, you said you wanted to meet with me again. Shit, Red, are you usually like this, or did Ben really knock all the memories out of you?"

Our last conversation materializes in my memories. It seems like ages ago, but it was only two days prior. So much has happened since he caught me in the woods and brought me back to his creepy cabin.

"No, I'm not usually like this, but as I said before, it's been a rough few days. I don't remember every conversation I have with a stranger."

Cameron makes a forced laugh and pushes himself back. "And I thought I just caught you at a bad time the other day. You really are a pain in the ass all the time."

"Excuse me, I am not a pain in the ass. You were the one who was rude to me, took me back to your torture dungeon, and then assaulted me in the park."

He leans forward. "Assaulted you? It wasn't... You know what, never mind. Are we done here?" He pushes himself back as if to exit the booth.

"Wait, no." I breathe out, my temper settling. Maybe I am coming on a little hot and heavy. "I do need to talk to you."

He shakes his head, an uncomfortable smirk marked across his lips. "And why should I talk to you when it's obvious all we do is argue?"

"Because I know you know more about the attacks, and I'm not giving up until I figure out what the hell is happening in this town."

I can tell he's trying to mask his expression, but I catch a bit of color drain from his skin. "Why are you so obsessed with those attacks?"

"Well, besides it being my job to investigate them, they've recently become a bit more personal."

He studies me. "What do you mean?"

I sigh. "It's hard to explain without sounding crazy."

"Try me." He leans forward, his dark gaze catching mine, sucking me into him.

I lean closer to him. Despite the magnetic pull, I don't want the sparse patrons of this coffee shop to hear me. "Do you know anything about werewolves?"

Surprise flashes through his eyes for just a moment before he pushes himself against the booth and laughs. "What kind of reporter are you, Red?"

I cross my arms. Sure, what I'm saying is crazy, but I'm picking up on his body language a little too well. He knows something. "Okay, then, how do you know Jack?"

A vein bulges at the side of his neck even as he steals his expression. "Family friend."

"Are you sure about that?"

He studies me before speaking again. "He's your boyfriend. Why didn't you ask him how we know each other?"

"He's not my boyfriend."

He scoffs. "Trust me, I know, but that's not what you said before he picked you up." He leans back and takes a sip of his coffee.

"I just said that because I thought you were going to lock me in those chains and murder me."

He laughs, and a devilish smile creeps across his face. "I told you those are for injured animals."

"Yeah, and I don't believe it for a second."

He shrugs. "Believe what you want."

"And to answer your question, Jack told me everything. He told me his real job and what roams in the woods you protect." He didn't tell me how he knows Cameron, but if what he says is true, maybe he's also a Werewolf Hunter. At least, it would explain the chains.

Cameron's calm demeanor snaps, and he grabs my forearm. "He's an idiot, and this is not the place to discuss it."

I hit a nerve without even saying much. My heart beats faster as I notice Cameron's strong hold on me, static electricity zapping me at the place of contact. I pull away, and his eyes clear. He lessens his grip, shaking his head slightly. He exhales. "I'm sorry, but if you really want to talk about this, we need somewhere private."

He gets up and throws a few dollars on the table. "Follow me back to my place."

Before I have time to respond, he's walking out the entrance.

I scramble after him. As much as I don't want to follow the asshole back to his house, I don't have a choice. He knows what's going on, and he's willing to tell me the truth.

19

A PULL

Cameron shuts and locks the door behind me.

I can't believe I let myself end up back in his weird torture cabin. He's had plenty of time to murder me and chop my body up in a million little pieces, but I can't help the fear that zips through my veins whenever I'm near him. I don't know if I should trust him, but some part of my brain can't help but want to discover more.

I scan around the cabin, this time noticing the more homey qualities of the place. Stacks of books rest on the side table, the coffee table, and by the fireplace.

Flannel blankets drape over the leather couch facing a window, looking out to the expanse of trees. Hints of cinnamon and freshly baked cookies linger in the air. Maybe my recollection of this place is a bit more frightening than the reality. My eyes meet the chains adhered to the thick wooden pillar at the far end of the living room, and my comfort washes away. Yep, still creepy.

I turn my attention toward the kitchen once I hear the clicking of glass.

Cameron pours himself an amber liquid into a low-ball crystal cup.

"Isn't it a little early to be drinking?"

He throws his head back, and I watch as his Adam's apple bulges as he gulps down the alcohol. The sight of it makes my mouth water for some odd reason. He breathes out and shakes his head. "It's never too early with you, Red."

I roll my eyes, crossing my arms over my chest, before pacing the outside edge of his oriental carpet at the center of his living room. "Okay, well, now you have me here. What is it that no one else can hear?"

Cameron pours himself another small amount before walking toward me and perching on the armrest of a worn leather loveseat in the corner. "What exactly did Jack tell you?"

I take a deep breath. This will be the first time I repeat the words out loud, and I'm already shitting bricks thinking about the craziness about to leave my lips. "He told me he's a Werewolf Hunter, and the creature that almost attacked me in the woods was a werewolf. He said the attacks weren't just a regular animal attack, but some mythical werewolf fuckery." I stop, trying to catch his expression.

His face lay flat, and he moves from the armrest to the chair, setting his glass on the side table.

I suddenly feel like I'm in a therapy session, and he's about to ask me questions about my childhood to explain how I can be so crazy even to entertain such a thing. "I know, it's crazy, but I've known Jack my whole life, and he seemed very convinced this was the truth." I leave out the part about my family's involvement. I figure one small dose of insanity at a time.

"So, you don't believe him?" He leans forward, resting his elbows on his knees, his gaze intense.

I step closer to him, pulled by an invisible string. "Should I?"

The air thickens around us, and my heart rate hinges on his next words.

He shrugs. "It's not *all* true."

I step closer, my legs almost grazing his knees. "What part isn't true?"

"The werewolf part."

"Oh, right." I turn away from his gaze, embarrassed.

"They aren't the cause of those attacks, and they're not all bad."

It takes me a second to register his words. "Wait, what?"

"Yeah, it's just like humans. There are some crazy ones out of the bunch, but most werewolves are just trying to survive."

"Are you fucking with me?" My cheeks heat as I rest my hands on my hips.

He stands, and I gulp, looking up at his intense stare. "No, I'm not fucking with you. I'm not one to fuck around." He takes a sip of his drink before placing it down and moving closer, trailing his eyes down the expanse of me. "Well, not with the truth, at least."

My skin pricks with goosebumps. He's so close to me that I can feel the heat radiating off his body. He's not saying anything worth swooning over. Besides being devastatingly handsome, there's no reason why my body should have this reaction to him. Okay, I guess that's reason enough.

I step back, shaking my head and remembering myself, remembering I just got fucked into oblivion last night by Jack. We're not exclusive or anything, but I'm not the kind of girl to put myself in these kinds of situations with two guys in less than twenty-four hours.

"So werewolves are real, but they had nothing to do with the pile of bodies that littered the forest floor or the giant beast that almost ripped my throat out? Something else is to blame for the almost unexplainable atrocities happening in this town. The werewolves are a bunch of kind-hearted citizens. I find all of this harder to believe than the fact of their existence."

He sighs and shrugs, turning away from me. "Believe what you want."

Anger mixes in my veins, and I rush toward him, stepping in front of him and grabbing his arm.

"That's not good enough for me. It doesn't make sense, and you know it. Stop with all the cryptic messages and tell me the truth."

He looks down at my hand, holding his wrists. When he returns his stare back to my gaze, it's like his eyes take on a different form entirely. They're dark and frightening, and I suddenly remember that I still don't know Cameron well enough, and Jack told me to be careful with him. I'm alone in his cabin in the middle of the woods. Not to mention the fucking chains adhered to his walls. Maybe I've gotten a little ahead of myself, but I don't soften and pull away as his gaze devours mine.

He smirks and bites his lip before leaning into my ear. His warm breath sends shivers down my spine. "I think you need to be a little more careful about how you sink your teeth into this story. Especially so close to the full moon."

He moves away from my neck but keeps his lips just inches from mine.

Something comes over me—a pull toward him, my blood thickening. My eyes fall closed as Cameron's heat burns me, and he removes the space between us, crashing his lips against mine.

He tastes like alcohol mixed with pure, unadulter-
ated pleasure.

I part my lips for him, and he kisses me deeper—electricity burning my nerves and traveling down
my body until it reaches my core. My bones turn to
liquid, and I lean into him, feeling the hardness of
his entire body. I've been with men before—obvious—one a little too close to comfort in time, but
something otherworldly shoots through my veins. It's
like molten lava mixed with steel. My heart beats wildly, and I feel like I can pick up a car.

His hands move to my lower back, and he pulls me
into him as his tongue moves against mine, and his
length rubs against my abdomen.

I'm lost in the moment—well, almost. A spark of
reason blares in the back of my mind just as I'm about
to give myself over to this beast of a man; I snap out of
his trance and pull back just as his fingers graze at the
bottom of my T-shirt.

"What the fuck?" I gasp as my lips pull away from
him.

His confused expression searches mine before a wall
of falls over his face. "You seemed to be enjoying it."

He steps away from me, picking up his glass again and downing the rest of it.

I rub my arms, completely uncomfortable. "I needed you to confirm what Jack said, and you've done that. I don't need anything more."

He sits back in his leather chair, his legs spread wide. "I don't think that's true at all. It definitely didn't taste like it." He smirks up at me.

It takes everything in me not to smack the shit out of him—or climb onto his lap, pull out his cock, and ride him until I forget everything that's happened over the last few days. No. No. Neither would get me anywhere.

I turn away, unable to gaze at him for another second, and charge toward the door. "Well, thanks for the coffee," I say as my hand meets his doorknob.

"Red," he calls before I've stepped over the threshold.

I turn back to him. His gaze softens, and he leans forward in his chair. "Just remember what I said. Most werewolves aren't bad. There's so much you still don't know."

My heart beats in my chest. This just confirms everything I thought. Cameron knows more than he's letting on to. I shouldn't leave. I should demand he tells me everything he knows so I can figure out what the fuck is going on once and for all. But I know if I stay, that's not going to happen. There's something weird between us, and I can't deal with that right now.

"Goodbye, Cameron," I say before shutting the door behind me.

20

TUNNELED INSIDE

"Red, is that you?" Granny calls as I step through the front door. It's already two in the afternoon, and I brace myself for the tongue-lashing I'm about to receive regarding my disappearance and late return.

"Yeah, it's me, Granny." I walk into the kitchen to find Granny sitting at the table, a cup of steaming tea to her side and an impressively long knitted scarf resting next to her folded hands. Her eyes study me with a disappointed tint coating her expression.

I don't let her speak her scoldings. "I'm so sorry, Granny. I've been investigating this story, and it's taken me on a whirlwind." I pull out a chair and sit across from her. "I ended up staying the night at Jack's because of that storm, and then on my way home, I had to follow this crazy lead."

Granny just shakes her head. "I don't like this, Red. I have a bad feeling about you getting tangled into this."

"What do you mean?" Jack said Granny was also a Werewolf Hunter. He said she'd forgotten everything, but maybe something deep inside her will reveal the truth.

She grabs my hand and sighs. "I don't know how to explain it. Just when you didn't come home last night, I knew you were in trouble. You're a grown woman. You don't have to update me with your schedule, but something doesn't feel right about you going after this story."

I nod and look around the kitchen, trying to think of a way to keep Granny talking and maybe reveal more about my family's history. My eyes meet a family portrait of Mom, Dad, and me. I stand, grab the picture, and bring it back to Granny.

I look down at the faded faces of my young parents. They were both so beautiful—never growing old and experiencing the harshness of time.

Granny leans over my shoulder, looking at the picture with a teary smile. "You're so much like your mother, you know. She was always putting herself in danger for what she believed in."

I study her face. "Oh yeah, like what?" Maybe this is it. Maybe Granny will remember my mom marrying a half-werewolf.

Granny sits up straight, a smile illuminating her face. "She was always causing a ruckus at school. She almost orchestrated a walkout when the school board announced they would cut the arts program."

I smile and lean forward. "I never heard about that. What else did she do?"

Granny smiles at me, her lips parting as if she's about to reveal more, but then a wash of concern drops over her expression. "Your father."

My heart speeds a beat. "What about my father?"

Granny just shakes her head. "For some reason, the memory is fuzzy, but I remember your father being dangerous, but that can't be right. I loved your father." She puts her head in her hands, rubbing at her temples.

I rub her back. "It's okay, Granny. Just tell me what you remember."

"Danger," she mouths, her eyes blank.

I lean in. "Danger from the werewolves?"

Her head darts in my direction, fear strew across her expression. "Don't trust them. Danger. You can't trust them!" She yells. Her eyes roll back, and her body slumps, convulsing against the chair.

"Granny! I shout, grabbing her and directing her to the floor. "Granny, what's going on?" I yell, tears blurring my vision.

"Don't trust them. Don't trust them," she repeats over and over. Foam seeps from her mouth, and I roll her to her side so she doesn't swallow her tongue.

I fumble with my phone from my pocket, dialing 911. The moment the operator picks up, Granny stops yelling, and her body stills. At first, I think she's dead, but I check her pulse and her breathing—normal. The operator tells me an ambulance will be here shortly. I hang up the phone and study her, tapping

her gently to see if she'll rise, but she remains unconscious.

Granny has never had a seizure before. She's getting older, and of course, more complications come
with age, but what are the odds that her first seizure
happened after bringing up werewolves for the first
time? I pray to every god in the universe that nothing
permanent is wrong with Granny, but I fear the ambulance and doctors won't be able to give me a reason
for the episode. Only one person comes to mind who
could know what happened. I pick up my phone and
dial his number.

21

RAZOR SHARP

Granny rises before the ambulance arrives, with no memory of her episode. "Oh, Red. You didn't need to make such a fuss. I'm fine!" She scolds me when I help her to the chair and let her know help is coming.

The paramedics check her vitals, and she rolls her eyes as they ask if she knows the current president's name. "I'm old, not stupid," she barks, crossing her arms over her chest.

"Granny, they're just making sure you're okay," I say, placing my hand on her shoulder, apologizing with my eyes to the paramedic kneeling before her.

Jack rushes through the door, his chest heaving as if he ran the whole way here. "Is she okay?" he asks as I approach. He places his hand on my cheek.

My skin pricks, and I take a step away from him, my cheeks heating. "She's fine, but it was so scary." Tears push at the corner of my eyes again.

Jack ignores the distance I'm attempting to create, grabbing my arms and pulling me in. "I know, I'm so sorry." He murmurs into my hair. I revel in his warmth for a moment, feeling safe in his arms before pulling away. "Can we talk privately?" He nods, eyeing the paramedics sprinkled around the kitchen before leading me up to my bedroom.

I shut the door behind us.

"Wow, this place hasn't changed a bit." He grins, looking at my paisley comforter and old band posters plastered on the wall.

I'm reminded of all our late study nights, stuffing our faces with chips and flicking erasers at each other. I smile. "Yeah, Granny isn't big on change, and I haven't been back since I left five years ago." Guilt swirls through my veins. Granny always visited me for holidays without a fuss. What if she had this seizure on her own? Maybe it's good that I told my work I need some time off. Not only to discover more about my family's history and bring to light the cause of the heinous murders happening in this town, but to make sure Granny is okay. I don't know if she can continue living independently anymore.

Jack must notice the worried expression on my face because he breaks the distance between us, holding me in his arms again. "The paramedics said she was okay?"

I nod, letting my body melt into his. "Her vitals are fine, and she seems back to herself." I push back. "Jack, she started yelling and convulsing when I mentioned werewolves."

"Did she say anything?" His eyes study mine, and I can't help but notice the nervous dart of his gaze.

"She just kept saying *danger, you can't trust them* repeatedly." I crumble into him again. "The werewolves must have really hurt her. She doesn't remember anything. Anytime I try to get her to recall the events of my parents' murder, she turns blank and spews information as if it's been fed to her. Now, she's having seizures when I mention werewolves. God, I don't know what to do."

He rubs my back. "It was good you were here, and now you know the truth about werewolves and your parents' murder." He pulls back, grabbing my hands. "Maybe you should stay in town for a little while longer to make sure your Granny's okay."

I wipe my tears away and straighten myself out. "Yeah, I was thinking the same thing. But while I'm here, I want to help. I don't think I want to kill werewolves, but I want to help expose them, maybe hold the information over the police so they will do something about the attacks. They obviously know something about the werewolves and are covering up their murders. Maybe we can get the army involved. I'm not sure, but I can't do nothing and let this continue."

Jack shakes his head. "I don't know if that's a good idea. The werewolves are hunting you. You should just let the Hunters take care of it."

"You mean like how you all took care of them before they murdered those people in the clearing? Obviously, whatever you all are doing isn't enough."

"It's not that simple. We don't know the identity of werewolves except for one family that the police won't let us touch. It's all part of some shitty alliance that they think will help keep the peace. The werewolves don't attack citizens, the Hunters don't attack this one family, and the police keep everyone in line. It's bullshit, but the Hunter Board hopes that from the bodies in the clearing and now you being targeted, they'll let us do something about it."

I step forward, determination lining my voice. "Great, then let me help. It's clear the police are protecting the werewolves, and need some persuasion. I can threaten to notify the nation."

Jack grabs my wrists, shaking his head. "No, the police would tell the werewolves and put you in even more danger. Focus on Granny. Let me worry about the rest." He presses into me. "Besides, maybe this could mean we could try us." He searches my face.

My heart hammers, and words lodge in the back of my throat. I don't know what to say. Here we are, in my childhood bedroom—Jack confessing that he wants to be with me. It's everything I ever dreamed of, except I'm not the same girl I was five years ago. I don't know if I want to be his shadow, remaining quiet in the background. Thankfully, Granny interrupts our awkward silence, screaming from downstairs. "Red, tell these people to get out of my house!"

I sigh and move away from Jack. "We'll talk more about this later."

He nods and follows me out of my bedroom.

***

"I need to start making dinner," Granny says once the paramedics have left, and it's just Jack and I at the kitchen table.

I pop to my feet. "No, Granny. You need to take it easy for the rest of the night."

"They said I was fine!"

"I know, but they also said you need to rest. Let me pick up some pizza." I walk toward the front door, trying to leave before Granny can protest.

"Do you want me to go?" Jack asks, standing.

"No, I want to go. I need to clear my head for a little." I grab my keys from the key ring. "Just stay here with Granny. I'll be back in ten minutes." I charge out the door, sighing in relief once it's shut behind me. The thought of living with Granny back in my hometown, which caused me so much pain, tightens my chest. If I can do something while I'm here, like help the Hunters, I'd feel better about being back. I'd have a purpose, but with Jack insisting that I can't get involved, I feel as useless and trapped as I did when I was sixteen.

I make my way to my car, parked in the grass far down the winding driveway. I decided to park farther away from the house to give Granny enough room if she needed to leave to go to the grocery store in the morning.

The sun hides behind the canopy of trees overhead, making shadows shift around me. I walk to the driver's side door, fumbling through my collection of keys before finding the right one. A bush shakes from behind me, and I whip my attention to the source of the sound, stepping forward a few feet out of instinct. Nothing.

A growl tickles the back of my ear, and the hair on the back of my neck stands straight. Something in my gut turns to stone, as if a force inside me knows exactly what lurks behind me. Before I can react, I'm thrown to the ground, banging my head on a rock.

I groan, barely conscious, as I roll onto my back—clenching my head. My vision clouds, but before everything goes black, I make out two grey beasts with glowing red eyes glaring down at me—their razor-sharp fangs closing in on me.

22

ON MY OWN

The space around me materializes slowly. First comes the slow trickle of sound—voices whispering from a distance. Then comes the awareness of my body—the pounding in my head, the cold pressing against me. My eyes flutter open, but absorbing the space around me takes a second. It's dark, but light flickers from lanterns outside my cell, illuminating the stone walls and tunnels leading away from me.

My cell.

The bars separating the small cavern I'm lying in reveal my imprisonment. I shoot up to a seated position, ignoring my body's nagging pull to rest more.

"Hello?" I call, immediately regretting my words. Why would I want anyone who put me here to come to my aid? No one puts someone in a cage to have a peaceful little chat, but my brain still isn't working at one hundred percent. I'm operating purely on instincts, which tell me I need someone to explain where the fuck I am and what's going on.

"Hello?" I call again, against my better judgment.

Darkness ripples from the far end of the hallway. I rise to my feet and lean forward until I can make out the three black-cloaked figures walking toward me. My heart pounds in my chest as they grow closer, their faces not becoming any more visible.

"Who are you?" I ask, my voice shaky.

They don't respond; they just continue their descent until they reach my bars.

"Um, hello? Who the hell are you guys?"

A voice booms from the middle figure. "You are Mildred Hoodson, daughter of Charles and Sophia Hoodson."

I wait for a moment, the air growing thick in the silence. "Uh, yes. I know who I am. Who are you? And why the fuck am I in a cage?" I step closer, anger slowly replacing terror.

A voice lower and more frightening than the first comes from the figure on the right. "Your mother was a Hunter, and you seem to be fulfilling her legacy. You are a danger to us all."

"A danger to you all? Look at me! Do I look dangerous? I think there's been some sort of a mix-up." I lean closer, wrapping my hands around the bars.

"You killed one of our own in the clearing. You have been seen with Hunters."

"What? No, I..." My mind registers what these mysterious figures' words must mean. They're werewolves. I back away from the bars.

"I promise I didn't kill anyone. It wasn't me." Werewolves kidnapped me from Granny's. My mind races with worry about her, but then I remember Jack was there. Werewolves wouldn't get to her with him in the way.

"You will have a trial in three days' time—the day after the Blood Moon."

"Are you going to kill me?" I ask, finally realizing the gravity of my situation. This whole story seemed too far-fetched—too impractical to be scary, but now that I'm behind bars, captured by werewolves, I realize why Jack didn't want me to get into this mess.

"Wait!" A man's voice bellows down the long corridor.

The three figures turn toward the source.

I don't move, unsure if I want to know what this new arrival could bring.

The man jogs into view, his features illuminated by the golden glow of the lanterns. "You've got the wrong person," he says, slightly out of breath.

"Cameron?" I ask, lunging forward. "Are you part of this?"

His frantic gaze catches me for a moment before he addresses the figures. "She doesn't know everything. She couldn't be the person who killed Leroy."

The figure on the left hisses, pulling down his cloak to reveal the back of a furry head and animal ears. He seems to be partially changed—his body a man's, while his head is almost wolf-like. I don't know shit about werewolves, but it seems that the transformation isn't always immediate. Maybe the Blood Moon has something to do with it?

"We will decide her innocence before a trial. Until then, she stays here. You know the rules." He flips his hood up again before all three walk away from my cage and descend back to where they came from.

Cameron stands in place, still catching his breath and staring at me.

"What the fuck is going on? Are you working with werewolves?"

He studies my face, wearing a curious expression. "Red, isn't it obvious?"

"What?" I strain my eyes, making out the dark stubble lining more of his face than usual. His eyes blink with gold, and his teeth point out sharply. I back away from the bars. He's turning. "You're a werewolf?"

"I thought Jack would have told you, and after our conversation the other day, I thought it was obvious." He shakes his head. "Well, now you know. I need you to stay calm. You've got yourself tied up in a fucked up situation, but I'll try to help."

His words don't reassure me. My mind races, replaying the conversations between Jack and Cameron over the past few days. Of course, Cameron's a werewolf. That's the dark history between him and Jack, and that's why he was so insistent on the werewolves' innocence.

Cameron seems to want to help me get out of this, but if everything Jack said is true—which it's looking that way—I can't trust him.

I'm not sure why the werewolves wouldn't just eat me on the spot and get it over with, but maybe they have worse plans for me. Maybe they're using me as a bargaining chip.

"Red, are you listening to me? You need to stay calm. I'll work on getting some evidence together for your trial, but you..."

"Why should I trust you?" I snap. "Your kind tried to attack me. You're a monster."

A wounded expression spreads across his face for a moment, but a cold and calculating demeanor quickly replaces it. "You're right. You shouldn't trust me. It seems the rumors about you are true—the Hunter blood runs deep in your veins, but right now, I'm the only person here who gives a damn if you live or die, and honestly, my concern is dwindling. You need me."

"I don't need you! Jack will come for me," I yell back, hoping that if I say it loud enough, I'll start to believe it.

He sighs and shakes his head, running his hands through his dark hair. "You're right. I'll just leave you to it then. Enjoy imprisonment." He winks before turning and walking down the cave hall as if taunting me.

I hate the way my body feels whenever I'm in his presence, as if lightning zips through my veins. Maybe it's my Hunter instincts preparing me for a fight, but it always leaves me feeling scratchy whenever he's gone.

I sit down, itching at my arms and thinking about what a smug asshole Cameron is. The thought of punching him in the face is a good distraction from my dire situation, but once my brain quiets and I realize just how utterly alone I am in this strange dungeon, I start to feel more sorry for myself.

What did I do? Did I just push away the one person who could help me? No, Jack will come for me. I'm sure of it. But even as I tell myself this, I can't help the doubt that shoots up my spine.

I've never been the type of girl to wait around for someone else's help. I may be in a monster prison, but I'm not helpless. It's time to think of a way to get the hell out of here—on my own.

23

APPARENT FREEDOM

T he concept of time doesn't exist while trapped in a dungeon. Usually, an escape mission happens in the dead of night, but the sun could be perpetually absorbing the planet right now, and I would have no idea.

I'm not sure how much time has passed, but after three meals brought to my cell by more cloaked figures, I have a better understanding of when the prison should be less occupied by guards.

I wait for what I assume is nighttime—although I imagine werewolves could be nocturnal, making it likely to be daylight. It doesn't matter—as long as I can escape without turning into kibble.

A smaller figure delivers my last meal of the day. I hope its size relates to its age and experience and that he's a young pup just starting his career as a monster overlord.

There's no slot in the bars to slide the silver tray of some mystery steamy mush into my cell. The prison door must be propped open for every meal, and the food must be placed on the floor. This seems like a serious design flaw for a paranormal prison. I'm probably the weakest creature they've had in one of these cells, and I plan to get the hell out of here. I can't imagine how difficult it would be to feed a Bigfoot or something without it ripping off the deliverer's hands. Maybe werewolves aren't known for their intelligence. I sure hope so because that's the only thing I've got going for me.

"Stand back," a squeaky voice comes from the black abyss under the cloak. The only sign telling me he's a werewolf is the pair of golden eyes shining through the void.

"Whatever happened to good afternoon or a simple hello?"

The figure doesn't respond.

"Alright then. What's on the menu today?" I walk closer toward the bars—my eyes lifting as if to gaze at the contents of the tray. The werewolf opens the door just as I conveniently trip, the door banging my shoulder as I hit the floor.

"Oh, shit!" he yells in his prepubescent voice. His feet scuff the ground, and I cry out in pain as I throw my arm overhead, carefully lodging a stone in between where the door would meet the stationary bars. I silently beg any god listening that my performance and the low dungeon lights will be my saving grace.

I hold my head at an imaginary injury. "I hope you have some good dungeon insurance because if I have any brain damage, I'm suing."

He scoffs before outstretching a hand to help me up.

I look up at his offering, honestly surprised at his gesture. A small pang of guilt rings through me, realizing he's going to be drowning in shit once I get out of here, and he's to blame.

"You're pathetic."

That pang poofs from existence.

"Sorry if I'm not at optimal efficiency after getting knocked out and locked in a cage." I crawl to my feet. "The lighting in here can't be up to code. You're lucky I didn't bang my head and spill my brains all over the floor." I charge toward him, pointing my finger toward his chest.

My explosive confidence startles him, sending him backward and tripping over his long robe. He catches himself on the bars. "You're in prison. Stop acting like you have rights," he says as if trying to convince himself of his words before shutting the door to my cell and turning to walk away. It's obvious I've rattled him, and he's embarrassed by his loss of composure. He quickly retreats down the tunnel without making sure the lock clicked into place.

I wait until his footsteps disappear before I reach out to check the door. I push it slightly, and it creaks open. "Yes!" I whisper to myself. I stop my quiet celebration to be sure that no one runs down the hallways or a booby trap doesn't fall from the sky. After a moment of silence, only interrupted by the dripping of water, I take a deep breath and push the cell door open, stepping one foot outside. I stop for a second, assessing my surroundings before charging toward a parallel tunnel.

This plan is as spotty as a slice of Swiss cheese. I have no idea where I'm running, and I could very well stumble upon a whole litter of werewolves sitting at a table, ready for their next meal, but what other choice do I have? I can't just sit in that cell waiting for someone to rescue me.

Although I hoped my escape plan would work, I'm surprised at how well it's going. I nearly shit my pants once I notice the fluorescent red Exit sign overhead leading me to my apparent freedom. These werewolves really are peas for brains when it comes to kidnapping and storing prisoners.

I make a sharp right, my heart beating out of my chest, and come to a door. I stop and do that little catholic cross prayer thing over my chest that I've seen people do and steel my nerves before pushing the door open.

Bright light swallows me, and I clench my eyes before stepping out into the warm moisture. My eyes blink open, and I almost can't believe it—I'm outside. I've emerged from a cave, the door camouflaged to look like a stone surface. I sure as shit have no idea where I am in the dense forest, but I made it. I escaped on my own.

I have to remind myself that just because I made it out of the prison doesn't mean I'm free. There could be werewolves hiding behind every inch of this forest. I don't have time to look around and plan my best course of action. I sprint in the direction opposite of the prison cave.

With each step, I grow more confident. Maybe it really could be this easy. I saved myself, and I'm almost home. When I see the bend of a road off in the distance, I can barely contain the joy slipping through my pores. I'm only a few paces away when something falls against me, bringing me down to the ground.

I struggle, wiggling my way to turn and face my attacker, who tries to force my hands behind my back. I'm able to turn my head slightly.

When I see his dark hair and shining eyes, I groan. "For fuck's sake. Will you leave me alone?"

"Believe me, I'd love to," he says, turning me to him and collecting my arms over my head. "It's like you want to get killed or something," Cameron says through his teeth.

I try to knee him in the balls, but he blocks me with his thigh, pinning me in place on the forest floor. His touch heats deep in my skin. I'm pretty sure I'm allergic to werewolves because every time he touches me, I feel as if my skin is about to melt off. My blood bubbles in my veins as if I try just a little bit harder, I could get out of his grasp. It's a stupid idea, though.

He's a tall man and from what I've seen—well built, but his ability to mold me to his will is scary impressive. I guess that makes sense, though. He is a werewolf, after all. They probably have ungodly strength even in their human form.

"I'm trying to help you."

"From my point of view, it looks like you just tackled me to the ground, and now you're attacking me."

He rolls his eyes and huffs. "You are a pain in the ass."

I'm ready to argue more, but before words can slip from my lips, he picks me up and throws me over his shoulder. "Let's get you locked up and safe again," he says in an amused tone.

"You're crazy!" I yell, banging my fists against his solid back.

"I know. But you better be thankful because crazy is about to save your ass."

INFURIATING PLACE

I wake up in an annoyingly comfy bed. The extra plush pillow under my head—covered in my drool—makes me want to commit murder. I sit up, wearing the same shirt and shorts from yesterday, before chucking the pillow at the locked oak door. I grunt before throwing my feet over the side, ready to continue last night's mission of banging and yelling until Cameron lets me out of his suspiciously perfect bedroom. He doesn't have a single item out of place, and the rich green accents in the comforter and throw pillows go perfectly with the oak furniture. The walls are painted cool grey over rich wood paneling, and warm light seeps from the bedside lamp. The room beats the dungeon, but somehow, I would rather be back there than in this infuriating place that reminds me of how close I was to escaping.

Cameron ignored my screaming and scratching the entire way back to his cabin. He just flung his doors open, threw me on his bed, and locked me in here without another word. Although he's an annoying ass whenever he opens his mouth, I much rather have someone to argue with than a stone wall. I banged on the door for what felt like hours but finally allowed my exhaustion to win and collapsed in his bed, engulfed with his strong, earthy scent. I tried to plug my nostrils, but it was of no use. I went to bed thinking of nothing but Cameron as much as I tried not to.

"Let me out!" I yell, banging against the door. There's no clock in his room. I just hope it's an ungodly hour and Cameron's regretting his decision to take away my freedom.

The door swings open, and I jump, nearly tripping as I step back.

"Good morning," he says coldly. Dark circles underline his eyes—usually dark but now glowing amber.

It takes me a moment to catch my beating heart and stand straight with composure. "No good morning," I bark, charging toward him. He doesn't move; he just lets me remove the space between us, staring me down with an unmovable expression. "I hope you've come to your senses and are ready to let me go."

He sighs, running his hand along his stubble, now fuller than the day before, and looks down at me. I fidget under his gaze as if just now realizing he's a werewolf that could do much more to me than lock me in his room. My mind flips to the image of us making out in his living room just a few days before. I shake my head microscopically, erasing the mirage.

"I've come to see if you'd like coffee."

"Coffee?" I nearly spit out the words.

"Yes."

I cross my arms over my chest. "Yeah, why don't you take me somewhere to get it."

His lips curve into a slight grin, and he turns. "How about the kitchen?"

I don't move for a moment, honestly shocked that he's letting me leave his room. He sits at his kitchen table across from me, bringing one of the two coffee cups in front of him to his lips.

Maybe this is a trick. I wait for another moment as he shrugs and looks at his cell phone before taking another sip. I charge toward the front door, grabbing the handle and twisting it. Of course, it's locked.

"Honestly, do you think I'm stupid?" he asks, not looking up from his phone.

I don't answer, standing at the front door with my arms crossed over my chest. I don't know what to do next. He's clearly locked this place, so I can't leave. Maybe sitting down with him is the best way to get some answers.

"Fine!" I yell after several seconds, startling him and bringing his attention away from his phone before he pushes it into the pocket of his jeans.

"Fine?"

I march toward him and pull out a chair. "Fine, I'll have coffee with you." I sit down and bring the cup to my lips but then hesitate. "Did you poison this?"

He gives me a dry glare. "If I wanted to kill you, it would be far easier than the last meal I killed."

I nearly choke on my saliva. I hope his last meal wasn't human, but I don't feel like discovering that now. He's right, though. I'd be dead by now if he wanted me to be—unless he likes to play with his food. I sigh and pick up the mug, taking a small sip. The coffee is bold and gives me an ounce of comfort. I revel in it for a moment—if only to remind myself that I'm human and not a caged animal. I change my composure. Maybe we can have a civilized conversation. "So, would you tell me why you kidnapped me?"

He folds his hands on the table and stares at me. I almost look away—his gaze locking with mine and making me feel the whispers of that itchy feeling again mixed with a heaviness in my veins, but I stay strong, holding on to the invisible line that tethers us together.

"I've already told you."

I scrunch my face. "No, you didn't."

"It's for your safety."

"Okay... what does that mean?"

He leans in closer, his scent filling my nostrils. God, does this man bathe in his own personal cologne? "You've been accused of murder, and then, instead of waiting for your trial or allowing me to collect evidence, you broke out of jail."

"Ha, it's not jail." I slap my hands on the table. "If that were the case, I'd have the right to an attorney. Don't act like there was anything *normal* about my imprisonment. For all I know, your kind could have been fattening me up and getting me ready for your next meal."

A vein in his temple twitches and his nostrils flare. "You might not understand the operations of our society, but that's what happens when you decide to tangle yourself up in this mess. If it wasn't me who found you, then it would have been someone who wouldn't be nice enough to allow you to sleep on their Tempurpedic bed or make you a fresh cup of coffee."

"Okay, great!" I stand up. "Thank you so much for your hospitality and *saving me* or whatever, but now let me go. I'll just go get Jack, and he can protect me."

Cameron releases a disgusted laugh from the back of his throat. "Yeah, I'd like to see him try from even just a few of our pack."

I'm starting to realize why Jack hates this guy more and more. "I watched Jack defeat a werewolf with my own two eyes. He can protect me."

"So you were there during the murder. Do you know that the Were he killed was only a teenager?" Cameron stands, walking closer to me. "And to think I was going to help you."

A teenager? The thought does pull at my heartstrings. I hope he's just lying to make me feel sorry for him. "I didn't even know about werewolves at that point! Also, the thing was trying to murder me."

"It wasn't trying to murder you. The Blood Moon is a few days away, and he couldn't control his shit. He was likely trying to protect himself from the monster you were with."

I step closer to him, looking up at his stare full of hatred. "The only monster I see is the one keeping me prisoner. From what I witnessed, the werewolves have done nothing but hurt people. They killed my parents, you know."

He scoffs. "Oh my God, you're impossible. You'll believe anything you hear."

"What am I supposed to believe, huh?"

He reaches out, touching my chest. I flinch and try to step backward, but his other hand wraps around me, holding me in place. "You know what's true in your heart. I know you can feel it."

The lava pours back into my veins, every cell in my body ignites, and the blood in my body pumps too loud for me to gather any semblance of reason.

"Your father was part werewolf."

His words knock me out of my trance, and I muster all my strength to push him back. The minute his touch disappears from me, my reason clears, and I gather all my anger to finish this pointless conversation. "And my mother was a Hunter. I was trying to discover the truth on my own, but then I was knocked out and captured, and now here I am again with my freedom taken away from me. From how I see it, I think I know what side I'm on. Now, are you going to let me go or not?"

He stares at me without a word, as if waiting for me to read the answer on his face.

I storm to his room, needing to make as much distance between us as possible. I can't think clearly when I'm around him, and I'm starting to wonder if his effect on me is some sort of werewolf power to lure in their prey. "Fine, then. If you need me, I'll be in your bedroom waiting for you to make up your mind on how you'll eat me." I say before I slam the door behind me, but not quick enough because I hear his smug little ass say, "Oh, you'd like that, wouldn't you."

25

ELECTROCUTED

You never truly know how restless your mind can be until you're locked inside a room without entertainment for a few hours. What kind of psychopath doesn't have a TV in their bedroom? I shouldn't be too surprised since Cameron is a werewolf and a kidnapper.

I've already gone through all of his drawers and discovered he organizes his underwear by colors—again, psycho. I went through his closet and found an assortment of tennis outfits. The fact that he plays shocks me more than if I had found a string of human teeth. I can't imagine Cameron swinging a racket on a court in those tiny shorts. Okay, maybe I can imagine it—as much as I try to push the thought away once it swims down to my core. Tennis just seems too normal. He should be pillaging villages and practicing witchcraft—not coaching soccer and working on his backstroke with a bunch of retired women.

It only takes about two hours to snoop through all of Cameron's belongings, and it doesn't bring me any closer to escaping his room. My mind races, wondering how worried Granny probably is.

Jack would know that I'd been captured by a werewolf by now. My car is still parked in the driveway, and I have mysteriously disappeared. It's his job to handle shit like this, after all. So why is it taking him so long to rescue me? Maybe the other werewolves are pretending they still have me captured and are using me as a bargaining chip for more power? Or maybe they told him I escaped, and he's searching for me through the endless woods. Whatever the case, I hope he figures it out quickly because I'm so bored I'm about to smother myself with one of Cameron's pillows.

A knock sounds on the door.

"I hope you're here to kill me now."

Cameron cracks the door open, but I don't lift my head from lying flat on his mattress. "I was here to see if you wanted to take a walk, but I am feeling rather peckish, so maybe roasting you over a fire is a better idea."

I strain my neck to look at him, amusement dancing in his amber eyes. The sarcasm oddly puts me more at peace, even if he joked about eating me. It couldn't have been more than five hours since I saw him last, but he looks completely different. He has a full beard, and hair covers his ears, running down his neck. He's wearing a long-sleeved shirt and tucks his hands under his armpits, but I catch his long fingernails before he does. God damn him to look so hot even while he's obviously transforming into his monster self.

I sit up, crossing my arms over my chest and my tattered T-shirt I'm still wearing from— I don't even know how many days ago. "I don't know if you've seen yourself lately, but if you're trying to make a joke, now isn't the best time."

The light dims from his face, and he walks into the bedroom. "It's the Blood Moon coming up. It makes even the strongest of us turn without control."

This statement piques my interest. I know little to nothing about werewolves, even though their kind makes up a part of my DNA. I began this whole journey to find answers. First, it was about the attacks, and then it became more about my family history. I still don't trust Cameron as far as I can throw him, but maybe I should utilize my time in captivity to discover more. "Fine. Where are we walking?" I ask as I stand from the bed.

"Just around the property. It's not good for us to be cooped up here all day. But don't get any ideas about running away."

I straighten my smelly T-shirt. "Don't you know anything about reverse psychology? It's like you're practically begging me to run away." I walk into his closet, grab a cashmere sweater, and pull it over my head. I catch his glance—laced with something like disgust, or arousal—I can't make it out. He turns his head as if the sight of me in his clothes makes him want to vomit. Or jack-off. Again, I have no way of reading him clearly. I try to ignore him—even if I can't ignore his smell as it slips around me, peppering my skin with goosebumps. "I guess it would make sense since you're all wolfy right now. You probably want me to run away so I become a more exciting meal."

He sighs and turns away from the door to the living room as I walk toward him. "Although I *love* hearing your offensive assumptions about werewolves eating humans, it's getting a bit old. I'm tempted to prove you right just to shut you up."

"So werewolves don't eat humans?" I catch up with him as he walks out the front door, straining to read his face. The cool midday air wraps around me, making me feel less claustrophobic. As much as I hate to admit it, Cameron was right about it being a good idea to get out of the house. Maybe that's what he wants, though—me to feel more comfortable so I don't try to run away again. If that's the case, he's a bigger idiot than I imagined because it will take a lot more for me to develop Stockholm Syndrome than a brisk walk through the woods, regardless of how handsome he is.

"No, we don't." He pulls a pack of cigarettes out of his pocket, lighting one and bringing it to his lips.

"Ugh," I cry in disgust. "Do you really have to smoke right in my face? You know those things will kill you."

He squints at me with a smile. "Since when do you care about my health?"

"I don't. I just…" I stutter, trying to find my rebuttal.

"Save it. I don't usually smoke. It's just with the Blood Moon coming, it puts me on edge. Mix that with being around you."

"Oh, please." I hit his shoulder, electricity zipping through me the moment we touch. That's so fucking annoying, but maybe it's a reminder that I should avoid touching him at all costs.

I shake my head, ready to get this conversation back on track. "You said there were bad eggs in the bunch. Do the bad eggs eat humans?" Maybe these are the ones that killed my parents.

"Have you heard of Jeffrey Dahmer?" he asks, not turning toward me.

"Was he a werewolf?" Oh my God, I never thought that people I've thought were people could very well be a werewolf or a paranormal monster. The edges of my reality shake with questions.

"Nope. He's a human that eats humans. That's about how common it is for werewolves to eat humans."

"Oh." I'm kind of disappointed. I think I'd rather have all serial killers be monsters instead of fucked up humans, even if I am a fourth werewolf. Maybe it would make the universe seem less harsh. "Well, what do werewolves eat then?"

He finally looks at me, scrunching his brow in disgust. "We eat the same things you do."

"Okay, geez. How the heck am I supposed to know that?"

"Your father was Charles Hoodson, right? You're part werewolf. Have you ever had any cravings for human flesh or wild boar?"

"Just because my father was *supposedly* a werewolf doesn't mean I am. I mean, I know for sure I'm not. I'm just a regular human."

He glances at me curiously as if to say something but then shakes his head and continues to look straight ahead.

I peel myself away from the shade of our conversation to notice our path. Damn it. I should have been paying more attention to the surroundings of Cameron's cabin so I can escape later whenever I find a way to get out of his room. I've been in and around his house before—when I wasn't a prisoner, but I wasn't too focused on mapping out an escape route then. We're already deep within the woods, walking along a worn path. A creek bubbles in the distance, and birds chirp overhead, but I hear no signs of cars or civilization.

A thought blares through my consciousness, snapping me out of my survival mode. "Did you know my father?"

"Yeah," he says, not slowing his pace.

If he knew my father, he must have known about me. "Why didn't you tell me you knew who I was when I first met you?"

"I didn't know who you were until Jack arrived at my house. Then everything clicked into place, and at that point, I figured you were already brainwashed."

"I'm not brainwashed," I say with an edge.

"Whatever you say."

I take a deep breath. Cameron knew my father, the *real* version of my father. I need to know more. "What was my dad like?" I say, softening my tone.

"I was just a kid, but he's actually the person that inspired me to become the Human Liaison."

"Human Liaison?"

"Yeah, that's my position in the pack. That's why I'm the park ranger and participate in community activities. Only a few government officials know I'm a werewolf, but I need to ensure I integrate into society to keep the peace."

So Cameron is the person that Jack was mentioning couldn't be touched. Why the fuck didn't he tell me the powerful werewolf was Cameron? "And that's what my father did?" I don't even realize how close I'm walking with him now. It's like I'm inching as near as I can, as if I need his memories of my parents to seep inside of me.

"Yeah, that's how he met his mate, your mom. You really don't know anything about your family history, do you?"

I want to tell him that he's an asshole and that, of course, I don't know anything because his people murdered them before I ever got the chance to know them, but I'm too distracted. "They were mates?"

His cheeks blush, which is odd because in the short time I've known Cameron, he hasn't been one to show much emotion besides asshole-ness. "Yes, werewolves have mates. Well, not all, just the lucky ones. It's a pre-destined partner, and there's only one in a Were's lifetime. A Mate is your perfect match. It's something no one can control."

I don't mention that Jack already explained mates to me. I figure bringing him up won't keep this conversation moving. I don't know if I like the idea that my parents only got together because they were *mates,* but it explains why my mom would end up with a werewolf. Maybe I should think it's romantic that they were destined for each other, but I'd like to believe in love where there's a little more choice in the matter.

"And my father, the half-werewolf, half-human, found a mate with a human hunter?"

Cameron chuckles. "Yeah. Even though I was a little kid, I remember it being quite a big deal in the pack. I thought it was cool, though. It was like a real-life Romeo and Juliet situation."

"You know about Romeo and Juliet?"

He stops and glares at me. "I didn't grow up under a rock. I went to public school for fucks-sake!"

"Okay, okay, geez. Sorry, I don't know everything about werewolves."

"It's just that you know *nothing.*"

My cheeks heat. "Well, forgive me for having my parents *murdered* by werewolves when I was five years old. How the hell do you expect me to learn anything?"

He stops walking, his eyes softening as he studies me. "That's really what you think happened?"

I stop next to him. "Well, I used to think they died from a regular murder, but yeah, apparently, the reality is monsters murdered them."

He grabs my arm, electricity shoots through me, and I try to pull away. He doesn't let go. "Red, that isn't true. Werewolves didn't kill your parents. You need..."

"How can I trust you?" I yell, finally regaining ownership of my arm. "You were just a kid when they died. How could you know for sure? Besides, you have me trapped in your house as a prisoner. Why on earth would I believe anything you say?" I turn, picking up my feet to charge away from him. Trying to escape now is useless, but I must move my body. I need to create distance between us so I don't implode.

I only make it a whopping three steps away before Cameron pulls me against him. I'm pissed now, and I kick at his ankles and claw at his arms.

"Fuck," he mutters as he lifts me off the ground.

I continue my attack until Cameron trips, falling and bringing me with him. I squirm under his large body as he lifts himself up on his forearms. "Let me go!" I yell, now facing him.

He looks down at me, his expression completely calm as he shakes his head. I continue hitting his chest until he grabs my wrists in one swoop and brings them over my head. "Another step, and you would have been dead!"

"Just kill me already if you're going to keep threatening me."

His grip tightens, and a surge of energy flows through me. I push against his grasp, enough to break my hands free. His expression morphs into shock, and I can't tell if he's fucking with me or if I really just overpowered a werewolf on the brink of transforming.

"You were about to step on a rattlesnake," he yells before I have a chance to push him off me.

"What?" I ask, straining my neck to look behind my head. Sure enough, only a few paces away from where we lay, a brown snake coils in the center of the path, his tail rattling and his head perched, ready to strike.

"Oh," I say meekly, finally returning my eyes to him.

He sighs and shakes his head but doesn't move. My body relaxes, and I rest my hands against his biceps, not realizing it until my skin meets his. I gasp, feeling that same energy I felt moments before. This time, though, it's not clouded by adrenaline. It's as if I've been electrocuted but can't pull away from the source. My mind rushes with impossible thoughts. I could move mountains. I could defeat armies, but I don't want to move a muscle. All I want to do is revel in this feeling, to increase it—bring the sensation to every inch of my body.

Cameron's eyes lock on mine, and I can read everything behind them. He feels whatever I'm feeling, too. Fire dances behind his amber eyes, and it's like they're pulling me in—calling me to be consumed by the flames. I head to his siren song. My body slackens, but my grip grows tighter, pulling him into me.

He lowers his face, his lips just millimeters above mine. His hot breath fans my skin. His scent cocoons me, and it brings me near tears. I can't pull away. I might die if I do.

A bang bellows behind me, and it's as if a cold bucket of water drops on my head. I'm snapped out of whatever weird werewolf magic trick Cameron tried to pull on me. I push him away, startling him and making it possible to escape his embrace and stand to my feet. I search in the distance, looking for the source of the sound.

"It was just a branch," Cameron says cooly, getting to his feet and dusting himself off.

"How do you know?" I ask, holding my arms over my chest and unable to stop fidgeting.

"I know every sound in these woods. Especially now, with my senses heightened." He points to his ears, larger and furrier than before we started this walk.

"Oh."

An awkward moment of silence passes between us. I stare at the ground, just praying that a bear charges through the woods and swallows me whole.

Cameron clears his throat. "Well, we should probably head back. It's about to get dark."

I nod and begin walking in the direction we came.

After we walk for a few minutes in silence, I clear my throat to speak. "Thank you for saving me."

"Of course," he says, his eyes meeting mine—as intense as they were when he loomed over me on the forest floor.

I break his gaze and stare ahead. "I guess it's better for you this way."

"How so?"

"I won't be a great meal riddled with snake poisoning."

He clicks his tongue in annoyance. "Oh, my God, shut the fuck up." He runs his hand down his face.

"No. I'm still a prisoner. If I'm too annoying, just let me go."

"God, why didn't I let that snake bite you," he says up to the clouds.

I walk ahead, not wanting to be near him for another second. "From what I've seen, everything you do is stupid, so it doesn't surprise me." Maybe I'm the idiot, though, for thinking this time as a prisoner could be useful and I could learn more about my family's history. There's no silver lining to my captivity. My focus needs to remain on escaping.

26

RELATIVE RESCUE

"Where have you been?" The whole house rattles as the front door slams shut.

Someone's here. I'm unsure if I should be happy or terrified, but I jump from Cameron's bed, pressing my ear against the door to listen.

"Hey, wait..." Cameron yells to the unknown visitor.

"I've been blowing up your phone for the past two days. You can't pull that shit with the Blood Moon so soon."

I know that voice. I bang on Cameron's bedroom door. "Help!"

Silence.

"Cameron, what the fuck?"

Her footsteps pound before she stomps toward his room, fidgeting with the door lock and then swinging it open. "Red?" She gasps, confusion spread across his face.

"Carmen, you have to help me. He's kidnapped me."

Cameron steps in front of the front door, his hands over his chest. "I'm protecting you." He mumbles angrily.

"What's going on?" she asks, hands on her hips.

I shake my head, singling out a thought. "Wait, how do you two know each other?" The reality that maybe Carmen isn't my saving grace settles over me. Did she fuck Cameron too? Why does the thought make me angry? Maybe it's because he's obviously a psychopath.

"He's my idiot brother."

Brother? Then that means… "You're a werewolf?" I ask, finally paying close enough attention to notice the hair crawling down her neck and over her shoulders. Her eyes shine, and her glossy red nails are pointed into claws. I back away from her.

"Fuck, Cameron. You let the New York Times reporter know about us?" She rubs at her temples. "I need a drink." She walks over to the kitchen, pulling out his bottle of whiskey from the cabinet.

"The Council had her imprisoned. She's accused of murdering Leroy. She escaped, and I brought her here."

Carmen puts down her glass. Her eyes darken as she stomps toward me. "You killed Leroy? I knew I shouldn't have trusted you when I saw you with Jack."

I back closer to the bedroom door. Maybe Carmen's the sibling I should be more frightened of. Cameron walks between us, outstretching his arms. "Calm down. She didn't kill Leroy. I just need to gather evidence. I figured I should wait before going to the Council until after the Blood Moon. As we know, it tends to make us… short-tempered. He eyes Carmen up and down.

She takes a breath and steps backward. "Sorry."

I march forward, pointing my finger at his chest and staring him in his eyes. "No, that's not how this is going. I escaped prison, and then your brother kidnapped me and locked me in his bedroom."

He stares down at me, his nostrils flaring as if soaking in my scent.

My breath catches, and I fall a step backward.

"Okay, I see what's going on here."

"What?" I whip my head to Carmen, watching with a smile, and her arms crossed over her chest.

I step toward her with pleading hands. "Carmen, you need to help me. Your brother is crazy."

She dodges me, throwing her hands up. "Nah, I'm staying out of this. I'll just be on my way."

"What? I thought you were my friend. You're just going to let him do god-knows-what to me?"

She sticks her fingers in her ears. "Nope, I don't want to hear about what you two plan to do. I'll just be on my way. Bye, Doll. Love ya." She blows me a kiss before walking out his front door and slamming it behind her.

I stand stupefied.

Cameron chuckles next to me. "I see you're friends with my sister.

I glare at him. "So you're just from a whole family of crazy."

"Yep, I guess so."

"Ugh!" I screech, seething, before returning to Cameron's room and slamming the door. I don't miss the sound of the lock clicking into place behind me.

No one is going to help me get out of here. It's time I figure this out on my own.

27

AN ANIMAL

Maybe I didn't care much about escaping before. Maybe Cameron's wolfy voodoo numbed my brain and made me ignore the viable escape plan sitting right in front of me.

The window.

Of course, it's locked, but I know how to open it. Even as a bullied teenager, I'd had my fair share of breaking out of my bedroom window. Okay, I did it once, but that's enough to remember how to unscrew the latch to break free.

The memory from high school when Jack begged me to sneak out to join him at the country concert at the local pub floods my brain. Jack was my best friend. It was normal for him to ask me to hang out, but never at night. I'd been so excited to spend time with him that I didn't even care if I got caught. Thankfully, I got out my window and to the concert without a hitch, but I probably should have just stayed home. It wasn't the romantic night alone with Jack I had envisioned. I ended up in the back of his truck, squeezed between two other football players who were drunk and smelled like a urinal.

It's not like Granny didn't trust me and thought I'd sneak out. She was just paranoid and made sure the windows couldn't be opened from the outside, which ultimately made them unable to open from the inside. I wonder what Granny truly worried about crawling through my window. I guess it doesn't matter now because even with all of Granny's protectiveness, I'm still captured by the beast she feared, but it won't stay that way because I'm getting the hell out of here.

I'd hoped Cameron would have a drawer filled with bobby pins left over from past lovers. Okay, maybe I didn't hope for that. For some reason, the thought of Cameron fucking somebody bubbles my stomach acid, but bobby pins would make my escape much easier. Luckily for me, I found a nail filer in his bedside drawer.

I wait until the dead of night. I'm still unsure if Cameron's nocturnal, but I make my move when I don't hear him stirring for several hours. It's like riding a bicycle—all those tutorial videos from years before overriding my brain.

The last screw falls to the window pane, and I take a deep breath before pulling the window open. It's been shut for some time because an ear-piercing screech sounds as it slides to the top. My heart hammers in my chest, and I freeze, waiting to hear Cameron's footsteps outside my door. Everything remains silent, and before I can chicken out, I catapult myself out of the room and into the night air. I stumble onto the ground but jump to my feet, running without any idea where I'm heading. I know it's a stupid plan to run through woods filled with werewolves with no sense of direction, but it's the only one I got, and I'm not just going to wait like a sitting duck before the werewolves decide to kill me or use me as bait to hurt Jack.

The cicadas sing around me like tiny alarms, heightening the urgency pumping through my veins. Trees whip past my line of vision, some smacking me in the face as I push through. My pulse mellows when I've created some distance between Cameron's house, but then a howl sounds from somewhere behind me. I look back but don't see anything. Somehow, this unnerves me even more.

I keep running, ignoring when my T-shirt snags on a branch, nearly ripping it off my body. The howl comes again, this time closer. Maybe it's just a regular wolf. There must be regular wolves in this forest. But what if there are no such things as regular wolves, and all I've been seeing my whole life are transformed werewolves? I shake my head to rid the thought. It won't help me now.

Footsteps—or should I say paw-steps—come from behind the trees next to me. Whatever it is—it's gaining on me. A scream lodges its way in the back of my throat. I increase my speed and force myself to continue focusing on the jagged path before me, but it's no use—something pounces, tackling me to the ground.

Who am I kidding? I knew it was Cameron even before I turned around from underneath him and met his glowing amber eyes. It's like I can smell him. He should cut back on whatever cologne he's wearing, or he will have a harder time sneaking up on people.

Even though it's futile, I don't give up my fight and pound against his chest. He growls at me and grabs my hands—pinning them to the ground above my head.

"This again? God, you're so predictable," I say between clenched teeth, still trying to worm free from his grasp.

"I could say the same about you," he replies cooly.

"What's the end game to all this, huh? Why are you keeping me here? What is it going to take to let me go?"

"You need to stay until the end of the Blood Moon. My people are just and fair, but if they catch the prisoner that escaped leading up to the Blood Moon, it might not be as civilized."

"Then put me on a plane to New York. I'll leave this fucking town if you just let me go." I don't know if I believe my words. Could I really leave Granny or Jack without a proper goodbye?

The moonlight from overhead illuminates Cameron's shadowed features. He's shirtless, and it takes everything in me not to let my eyes wander past his neck. He's still human, but barely. His facial hair is completely out of control. His teeth have a little more of an edge to them, and his ears seem larger. I should be terrified of him, but for some reason, I want to fight—to see what he'll do when he loses control. I watch as his face shows the thoughts wrestling around in his head. I wait for a quick response as to why my plan won't work either. When one doesn't come, I realize he doesn't have one.

"Well?" I whisper, my breath suddenly heavy.

"I can't let you go." He shakes his head, not leaving my gaze.

His touch sears into my arm, and I'm suddenly aware of every inch of his body looming over me. He moves down, his lips just inches from my own.

"Why?" My eyelids droop.

He leans to my ear. "You know why." He growls.

And even though I have no fucking idea what he's talking about, my body sure does. Every cell ignites within me. All the anger and hatred toward him dissipates in an instant. It's like some primal creature inside me doesn't see him as a monster but as the answer to my every desire. I can't stop the moan that escapes my lips as I lift my body off the ground and press myself against him. The moment I touch him, his grip tightens, and he presses me down into the earth with his weight. His length rubs against me, and he doesn't make any attempts to hide it—he just grinds harder into my abdomen.

"You can't leave," he whispers, his lips hovering over mine.

"I'm here," I whisper back before straining my neck to capture his lips. His mouth devours mine—his tongue sliding between my lips, filling me.

I buck against him, feeling desperate to have his hands on my body, and it's like he can read my mind because he lets go of my wrists, bringing one hand down to my chest and the other he uses to cup my ass. The second my hands are free, I cling to him, wanting to explore the valleys and hills that run down his abdomen—to venture below his waist, but he's pressed so tight against me that all I can do is run my hands down his back.

He drops me to the ground, lifting himself and creating space between us. His hand runs down my side until it meets the waistband of my shorts, sliding underneath. "I've been waiting to get these off you the moment I saw you in that cage. I can smell him on you. Fucking smell him. Do you know how fucking feral that makes me?" His finger grazes my cunt, and I shutter. "I bet he can't make you this wet. You're already gushing for me."

His words turn my insides to liquid, and I can feel myself dripping down my thighs—down Cameron's fingers. He pulls his hand away from me, and I gasp. "Please," I beg.

He brings his fingers to his mouth, sucking and licking them clean.

I moan.

"God, you taste so fucking good." His eyes nearly roll to the back of his head.

"Cameron, I need..." I can't get the words out. I buck against him, needing the friction from his fingers, his body, his dick, any part of him at this point.

"Shhh, I know what you need." He brings his hand back to my core, sliding his finger through me.

"Yes," I yell, the pleasure starting from my toes and bubbling through me.

He inserts a finger inside of me, and I cry out. He smashes his lips against mine, and as he inserts another finger into me, I moan into him. "You feel so good," he says into my mouth. "So perfect and tight." He removes his fingers, running them up and down, growing higher every swipe, until he hits my clit.

I buck against his hand.

"So responsive." He hums and circles my sensitive bud.

"Cameron, I'm gonna..."

"Come. You're going to come hard for me, aren't you? Be a good girl, and come on my hand."

It's like his words caress every inch of me. A flower blooms inside of me, starting out light and small and bursting into a ray of bright colors. I claw at Cameron's back as I cry out, grinding against his hand. I'm not completely in my right mind, but I swear the ground shakes from underneath me.

Cameron moans into my ear, loud and forceful, as if my pleasure is as much his. He doesn't stop until my body slackens.

"Fuck, Red."

I don't let go of him. Even though my orgasm passed through me, I'm not satisfied. I'm ready to be devoured fully by this werewolf, but he pulls away from me, rising to his knees. He twists his body, his hands exploring his back.

Even though it's dark, I can see the red gashes across his back. I look down at my hands, blood dripping down my fingers.

"What the fuck?" I rise to my knees, moving closer to examine him. It's obvious from the blood on my hands that I'm the one to cause these wounds, but as I gaze upon the large gashes, it's clear that they couldn't be made by a human. No—an animal did this.

28

ONE FOURTH

"Red, stop; it's fine," Cameron says, looking over his shoulder and sporting a strained smile.

"It's not fine," I say, my voice high-pitched and my head buzzing with anxiety. "What the hell happened? How could I have done this to you?" I work on blotting the ten gashes down his back—made by ten nails—no, claws. He's covered with hair now—his transformation becoming more apparent. I'm so worried about the damage I've apparently done to him that I don't have time to examine how quickly I turned from hating this man to letting him fuck me with his fingers on the forest floor to fussing over his wounds as if it pains me as much as it does him. That's the funny thing about adrenaline. It doesn't give you the time to evaluate if your behavior is toxic or psychotic. I'm just running on pure emotions, which seem to shift second to second.

"I have a theory," he says, swiveling around on the stool and grabbing me from the back of my legs. He stares up at me and pulls me closer, his amber eyes full of hunger as he runs his hands down my thighs. The gesture is so intimate—too bizarre to come from the man who kidnapped me. He obviously isn't frightened of me. Could I nearly rip this man to shreds, and he'd still be willing to be near me? I will myself not to swoon at the thought.

My emotions change again, as if they're a nineties viewmaster and I just flipped to the next scene. I step away and watch as hurt seeps into his eyes, and his expression folds in on itself. I can't feel guilty. Yes, seconds ago, I would have contorted into a pretzel and allowed him to fuck me however he saw fit, but this isn't normal. I'm still his prisoner, and we both need a reminder of that.

"What's your theory?" I finally ask.

Cameron studies me for a moment longer before clearing his throat to speak. "It's not that difficult to put together, Red." He walks toward the kitchen, opens a cabinet, and grabs a crystal bottle of brown liquid.

I follow after him. "Enlighten me."

He looks up from his cup before taking a sip. It's still dark out but nearly morning. I don't blame him for drinking, though. I have half a mind to ask him for my own glass, but I don't want to derail the conversation. "Need I remind you that you're part werewolf?" he says.

"I'm a fourth werewolf."

"A fourth is a part."

"Okay. So what? I'm not a werewolf. I think I would know."

"So you've never shown any signs of powers, anything unusual?" He steps closer to me, his eyes trailing down my body as if I'm going to sprout a tail or something.

I step away from him. "No." Even as I say it, my mind whirls with strange instances. I replay the sensation of the ground shaking when I orgasmed. Could that be from me? Could the earthquake from graduation be from me as well? I decide not to mention it. It seems too outlandish, even for everything currently evolving. I've felt...different ever since I showed up in this town. I try to pin them in place and figure out when it happened. "I mean, sometimes I feel weird."

"When?"

"It's been a recent thing."

He places his drink on the counter and removes any possible space between us. I stare up at him, my heart hammering in my chest. The electricity I feel whenever I'm near Cameron surges through me. My mind fogs with the scent of him. It's like all my pores are tiny nostrils. My eyes droop. "When I'm near or touching you, I feel different—itchy but more intense. Like my nerves are reaching out to tether to something." I barely realize the words that pass through my lips.

He leans down, his mouth hovering over the shell of my ear. "I'm a werewolf. My powers are bringing out yours. The Blood Moon is tonight, heightening the effects. You're a werewolf, Red."

The words snap me out of my trance. I push him back, shaking my head. "No! You're doing this to me.

This is some sort of werewolf magic to lure me in. Jack told me all werewolves are evil. I can't be a werewolf."

His eyes blink wide as if my words stabbed him in the gut. "God, Red, your father was a werewolf. How can you say all werewolves are evil?" In a flash, his expression changes from hurt to anger, as if he's spent years mastering the art of making sure people don't see him in a vulnerable state, and I was able to crack into his mask for a moment before he brought his iron walls back down.

I turn away from him, rubbing my temples. "I don't know, okay. I barely knew my father. Maybe he was evil."

Cameron grabs my arm and twirls me to face him. "Why is it so difficult for you to see what's right in front of your face? I'm a werewolf, and I'm not evil. If I was, would I be trying to clear your name, letting you sleep in my bed, saving you from snakes, making you scream with pleasure?" He runs a finger down my cheek.

My skin peppers with goosebumps, and I turn away from him. He grabs my chin and brings my attention back to him. "You're a werewolf, Red. Maybe not as much as me. Maybe you don't show physical signs, but you have werewolf abilities. Don't think I didn't notice the ground shake when you came. You did that."

I'm shocked silent. Could I be a werewolf with powers to affect nature?

His lips lower to mine, and the electricity—no the power bubbles to life in my veins. I feel as if I could move mountains. My legs ache to jump. Strength surges at my fingertips.

I'm lost in the moment, but before Cameron's lips meet mine, I speak. "But Jack..."

He pulls away, hurt and anger in his eyes. "Fuck, Jack." He turns away from me, the veins in his neck bulging, and I reach out to grab him. "Wait," I say.

"No. Seriously. Fuck him. All he's been doing is filling your heads with lies, and it's not like it's his perspective or that he's ignorant. He knows he's lying. That crock of shit he told you about the attacks—your parents. I wonder what he would think if he knew the werewolf gene didn't pass you by."

"What do you mean he lied to me about my parents' murder? What happened?"

He stalks closer to me, anger radiating off of him. The sun rises behind him through the window, illuminating the hair growing down his arms. His teeth look more like fangs, and his eyes size me up as if I'm his next meal. I've always held fear for Cameron, but right now, my internal caution alarms warn me to back down. I step back, but he continues to move closer. "Would you even believe me if I told you?" He shakes his head before taking a deep breath and stepping back. "I can't do this right now. You infuriate me, and the Blood Moon is too near. I don't want to hurt you." He takes colossal steps backward as if he's afraid of me. "Stay in my room for the rest of the day. Take a shower. I'll bring you food to the door, but I can't see you until after tonight."

"But..." I try to reach for him.

"No. Stop. I can't," he pinches the bridge of his nose as if I disgust him, as if the smell of me repulses him.

I lift my armpit. Shit. Maybe I should take a shower. I'm suddenly embarrassed. I've been so focused on escaping that I honestly didn't give a fuck if I smelt good or not. Now, I feel differently for a whole slew of reasons I don't want to dissect.

"Okay," I say, turning toward his room. I can't believe I'm willingly going back to my prison, but now that I know Cameron knows more, I don't want to leave. I might also not want to leave due to the warm feeling racing to my core, but I'm now ignoring that part of myself. I need more from Cameron—in all ways possible. Tomorrow, I plan to finally learn the truth. I just need to survive this Blood Moon.

29

BINDS

God, why didn't I take advantage of Cameron's shower sooner? I spend over an hour letting the hot water pelt my skin from the rain shower overhead while contemplating the last few hours' events. The steam calms my nerves, and when I step out of Cameron's bathroom, attached to his bedroom, I feel like a new person.

There's a knock at the door, and I hold his white fluffy towel around me as I crack it open. Cameron's nowhere, but my eyes fall to the floor to find a pile of folded grey clothes and a plate of bacon and eggs.

I stand in the doorway, questioning if I should heed Cameron's orders about staying in his room all day or venture into the living space. I decide I still need more time alone, grab the items off the floor, and head back into the room.

I slip on the grey tank top and black biker shorts, trying not to spend too much brainpower wondering where Cameron got them from. Could they be left over from an ex? Why does the thought make me want to rip them off my body and burn his house to the ground? It must be a side effect of my new "powers" and the Blood Moon tonight; at least, that's what I'm choosing to believe. It's not like I can be jealous of Cameron having past lovers. He did yank off my clothes that reeked of Jack, a man I fucked just a few days ago.

God, my life is a mess.

I decide to focus my attention on my powers. I'm usually skeptical about the paranormal, but I'm starting to take Cameron at face value. Even though I hate to admit it, it seems to be the only plausible explanation for why I caused his injuries and the earthquakes that seem to follow my strong emotions. Maybe when he tells me the truth about my parents, I'll actually believe him.

I work on lifting Cameron's furniture to test my strength. I'm surprised that I can get his dresser off the ground a tiny bit without pulling a muscle, but my abilities don't seem ground-breaking. I wouldn't even place at a muscleman competition. Could I even call this sudden burst of strength a power? It just seems like I'm in better shape. Maybe being near Cameron triggers the results. That's the only time I've been able to do anything unexplainable or feel the buzz of energy running through my veins.

Looking at his bedside clock, I realize several hours have passed. I'm not tired even though I've exerted more energy than I have in a while, but I could go for something to eat. I press my ear against his door. I'm unsure if I hear Cameron, but it sounds like a wild animal struggling. Could other werewolves have come over? I open the door just enough to throw my voice. "Cameron?" I call.

"Don't come out here." He doesn't sound the same, but I sense it's him. I'm not sure if it's his smell or something more. God, am I going to start sniffing butts soon? I fucking hate this werewolf shit.

"Stay in the room," he says in a pained tone, chains rustling in the background.

"Are you okay?" A fear for his safety overtakes me, and I step into his living room. "What the fuck?" I exclaim as my eyes assess the scene before me. Cameron is chained to the wooden pillar in the far corner of his living room. He barely looks like himself anymore. Hair covers every inch of him, and his face is more animal than human. He's shirtless, only wearing grey sweatpants. His muscled chest and torso still look human but enhanced—bulging with muscles.

His eyes catch mine, and he yelps. He struggles with his hands chained behind his back as if his body isn't his own. "Get back in the room now."

My heart beats rapidly, and my brain separates from my body. It's like I can hear my blood thickening and pumping through my veins—a warm rush floods my core, and my skin prickles with goosebumps. My feet move on their own, bringing me closer to the beast. I have no idea what's going on, but for some reason, seeing him like this, almost completely in his werewolf form, makes me want to drop to my knees before him. "Cameron," I say breathlessly, moving closer to him. "What's going on? Why do I feel this way?"

He throws his head back against the wooden pillar. "Fuck! Red, I told you to stay in your room. It's the Blood Moon. I can't control myself fully, especially not around you."

"Well, I don't think I can either." I'm inches away from him now. I reach out my hand to touch his chest.

He hisses as if I'm branding him. "I thought this could happen. I'm sorry, Red. Just stop and go back to your room."

I run my hands up and down his chest. The feel of him under my fingertips nearly sends me into a spiral. Energy surges through me. I lean into his ear and whisper. "I can't, and I don't want to." I bring my lips to his furry skin, kissing down his neck.

He moans. "Fuck, Red."

"I want you," I say. I'm aware I'm not completely in control of my body. A part of me knows that if I tried hard enough, I could stop myself. There's still an ounce of reserve in me where, if I focused all my energy, I could fling myself back into his room and stop this, but that's the last thing I want to do. I've never thought I'd be so attracted to a monster, but seeing Cameron like this makes me want to fuck him until there's nothing left of me.

I bring my lips to his, sliding my tongue over his bared fangs. He gives into me, and his tongue—much larger than normal––slides from his mouth and into mine. My hands wander over his body, feeling the rock-hard muscle under the coarse fur. I press myself against him, even as my hands trail lower and lower until I reach the waistband of his sweatpants.

"Red," he says with a growl, warning coating the word.

"I want to feel you."

He yanks at his chains, his muscles straining from under me. "I can't...I can't control myself, but God, I want this so bad."

I dive my hand in, sucking in a big gulp of air as I feel his length, hard and impressively large under my fingertips. A gurgled moan mixed with a growl escapes Cameron, and I catch as his eyes nearly roll to the back of his head.

The power surging through me grows brighter now. I don't know if it's my abilities or if just watching Cameron—a monster, helpless to my touch makes me feel like I could rule the world. My fingers trail from the tip of him, lightly grazing over his bugling veins as I drop my touch lower and lower. When I reach his base, I gasp. My eyes shoot open to Cameron's watching me. "I'm not like a normal man. I have extra parts." His tone is apologetic.

"I don't want *normal.*" I caress the two bulges, wetness flooding me as I do. "What is this?" I whisper in his ear.

"It's my knot."

Of course. I know what a knot is. I wouldn't think something like this would do it for me, but I grind my hips against his leg, unable to contain my arousal.

He catches his voice. "This is why we need to stop. I can't control myself, and once I start I…"

"Shhh," I bring my finger to his lips. "Don't worry about me. I'm a big girl." I kiss down his jaw, his fur scraping against my skin, as I lather my palm in the wetness at his tip before stroking down slowly until I reach his knot. My mind races for what it would feel like to have it inside after he releases—the tissue filling until solid and unable to be removed from me. The thought seems so intimate—so erotic that all my brain can focus on is making this newfound fantasy become my reality.

He shudders again, and my mouth waters. I drop to my knees and pull his sweatpants down until all of him is exposed. He's glorious. His cock stands proudly—so hard I'm sure it won't take much to have him sputtering out of control. The thought of making this monster lose himself sends another wave of power through my veins and to my pussy.

I bring my lips to his tip, kissing it gently. He growls, the sound shaking the windows around us as he pulls against his binds. Wood cracks from the force, but he's still chained. "Fuck, why didn't I use silver?" he mutters to himself, but I can't focus on his words. All my attention drives to the fullness of my mouth, and I roll my lips down his length.

His hips thrust into me, encouraging me to go deeper. I gag, realizing he's too large for me to take him. I wrap one hand around him, stroking in tempo with my mouth. My other hand sinks into myself, my wetness soaking my hand and making me slide through easily.

"Red," he yells. "I'm so close."

His words encourage me, and I increase the tempo of my strokes, both on his dick and on my cunt, pivoting my attention to my clit so I can reach my edge with him. I want him to come inside of me, even if it's just my mouth at first. I crave the taste of him running down my throat. All I can think about is his knot hardening—his body wanting nothing more than to stay inside of me—to breed me.

The wood creaks again, and his chains clink together as he roars, releasing warmth into me and filling my mouth until I swallow. My hand darts to his knot—now solid. I wrap my hand around the twin rocks, imagining what it would feel like against the walls of my cunt. My pleasure barrels through me at the thought. I cry out, not releasing the pressure on either of us until I've emptied every last drop.

Before my body even slackens, Cameron's words break through my euphoric trance. "Red, you need to leave now." He's more urgent than before. "I'm about to break through these chains. The Blood Moon is only an hour away."

I wonder if he feels what I feel because even as my orgasm passes, urgency fills me again as if I haven't found my release for ages. Sure enough, when I glance down, Cameron's length stands tall, eager for me to climb on and fill me again.

My mouth and pussy water, but Cameron's words stop me from reaching for him. "Red, no. We need to stop. I want you. It pains me, but I can't control myself. We still don't know your true power. We cannot let this be our first time."

My release must swat away some of my fog because I register his words. I understand what he's trying to tell me, even as my body urges me to give in to my desires. I stand, and as I step away from him, my head clears even more.

"It's going to be even more difficult for you tonight." His words are tortured. "Go to the cabinet. Get the bottle of brandy and finish it. Knock yourself out."

I nod, stepping back further and looking around like I had just been transported to an alien planet. "What about you?" I ask.

"I'll be fine. I tested this chain and pillar last year. I should be fine if you aren't in the room. But you need to go. Now!"

I sprint to the kitchen before I have a second to let the fog take over, pulling out the half-full bottle of brandy and rushing toward his room. I shut and lock the door behind me, falling to the floor and bringing the bottle to my lips, taking a large swig.

The liquid burns my throat, and I close my eyes as I will it to blur my thoughts. My chest heaves, and I rest my head against the closed door before taking another gulp. The warm caress of the liquid starts to numb my senses, but I'm not foolish enough to stop drinking. I'm going to need a hell of a lot more alcohol to stop myself from escaping my room and fucking a werewolf until I turn to mush.

30

WOLFY POWERS

I wake to the sounds of cries throughout the night. Strange noises seep into the cracks of the room and beg me to open my eyes and explore the source. The brandy does its job, and although a part of me begs to rise from bed and greet the beast, my body weighs too much, and my brain can't connect with my limbs to carry me. Even my dreams are blurry—flashes of fangs, claws, and pleasure ruminate through my skull. The morning can't come soon enough.

I'm aware of someone grabbing me—picking me up from my bed and throwing me over their shoulder. "Cameron," I call, even if my eyes can't focus on the person carrying me. I've been waiting for him to come for me. I wanted him to break through his chains and take me in the dead of night. Now, here he is, taking me away to swallow me whole.

The moment I'm put down again, my consciousness burns out. Darkness surrounds me, and I let it consume me, hopeful to wake in the arms of my beast.

***

Sunlight warms my cheek and tickles my eyelids. My head pounds like a motherfucker, but I can't help waking up. I sit, blinking slowly as I take in my surroundings. "What the fuck?" I say as I assess the mahogany furniture and the warm linens around me.

The bedroom door swings open, and there he is—holding two cups of coffee and an examining look on his face.

"How are you feeling?" Jack asks.

I don't answer at first. My brain rushes to assemble the missing pieces of how I ended up back in

Jack's cabin. The steamy events with Cameron until I downed half a bottle of brandy flash through my mind. I bend over, cupping my head in my hands.

Jack rushes to me, placing the cups of coffee on the bedside table and putting an arm around me. "Are you okay?"

I push his arm away without thinking. Something about his touch chills me. I meet his eyes to catch the hurt expression on his face. "I'm fine." My head pounds from the volume of my own words, and I rub my temples. "Well, I'm hungover as fuck, but other than that, I'm fine."

"Here, drink this. It will make you feel better." He hands me the steaming cup of coffee, and I take a sip, trying to focus on the warmth flowing down my throat instead of the nausea bubbling in my stomach. After a few gulps, my head clears enough to direct a line of questions. "Jack, how did I get here?"

He grabs my hands, holding them in his. "I rescued you last night. I've been hunting you for the past four days. I'm sorry it took so long to find you."

Fear drops through me like a torpedo, remembering Jack's title isn't "rescuer" but "Werewolf Hunter." "Where's Cameron?"

"Don't worry, he can't hurt you." He rubs his thumb over the back of my hand.

"Did you hurt him?" I can't hide the panic in my voice.

Jack gives me a quizzical look. "Do you not want me to hurt him? He kidnapped you and drugged you."

"He didn't drug me." I jump to my feet. "Just answer me. Did you hurt him?"

He stands, slowly stepping toward me and studying my face. "Did he use mind control on you? I know werewolves are capable of that. I swear if one of those disgusting animals got in your head, I'll rip out their innards."

I want to question why he failed to mention Cameron was a werewolf earlier or reprimand him for speaking so ill of werewolves, which I happen to be. Still, the only thing I can focus on right now is knowing whether Cameron's safe.

Jack was wrong about werewolves. Cameron is not evil. He chained himself to a pillar to protect me and used every ounce of his will to stop me from doing something I might regret in the morning. Even with the bright light of my hangover shining over my memories, I don't regret what I did last night. I was under some sort of Blood Moon spell, but I'd do everything all over again with a clear head. There's something between Cameron and me—something I can't explain.

I don't back down. "Jack, just tell me."

"No." His rough tone startles me. "He was chained to a pillar, knocked out. I broke into the room and found you. I didn't have time to kill him. I had to make sure you were okay. But the other Hunters will be there soon to try to finish the job. Him kidnapping you goes against everything in our alliance. The police protect the Human Liaison as long as humans in the area are safe."

I grab his arm. "Jack, you have to tell them to stop. You can't hurt him."

He shakes me off—repulsed, studying me before grabbing my arms. "Red, snap out of it. Werewolves are evil, disgusting creatures. He tried to kill you."

"No!" I pull my arms back. "How can you say that? My father was a werewolf."

"He was part werewolf, and I'm sorry Red, but your mother would be alive today if it weren't for him. Werewolves have evil in their blood."

I'm stunned, silent for a moment. I examine his features—his broad chest, his cut jawline, and the magnetic green in his eyes. A few days ago, simply being in his presence weakened my knees. He was my childhood crush—my best friend, and with just a few words, his novelty melts away. Maybe my otherworldly connection with Cameron is related to it, but I know that's not true. He just said my father had evil in his veins, which means he must think I'm evil, too.

I straighten my shoulders and stare him down. "I'm a werewolf, Jack."

He clicks his tongue and turns away from me. "Don't talk about yourself like that. Just because your father was less than doesn't mean you inherited those traits."

I can't believe the words coming out of his mouth. I try to replay our past conversations. Did he talk this way about my father before? Surely, even with what little I knew about werewolves, I would be repulsed by how he speaks.

I step closer to him, anger overtaking every emotion. "Well, guess what, Jack? That makes me less than, too, because I inherited those traits. I have powers all heightened by the Blood Moon." I point a finger into his chest and cock my head. "I guess I was right about you thinking less of me in high school. You just wanted to fuck me because I lost a few pounds. No matter what, I'll always be disgusting to you, but I promise you, you look a hell of a lot more hideous from where I'm standing." Maybe coming into my powers gives me some sort of wolfy dominance thing. I don't recognize this harsh self, but I don't hate it. Without letting myself waver or regret my words, I turn toward Jack's bedroom door to storm out and do whatever I can to rescue Cameron.

Jack grabs my hand, pulling me back to him. I capture his expression, not letting the rage leave my face; his is soft and defeated. Maybe I spoke too soon, and it's not what it seems. Maybe Jack cares for me and spoke rashly after days of worry riddled his senses. I soften, stepping close to him to hear what he has to say.

He relaxes his grip around my wrist and trails his fingers up my arm. "I'm sorry, Red. Werewolves killed my mom, and I'll never get over it. You're not disgusting to me."

My shoulders relax a bit, and I glance down at the floor. I sympathize with him. I know what it's like to want to avenge your parents. He may have his hatred misguided, but he's probably just acting on what he's been told his whole life.

"Sure, you have one disgusting trait, but I can ignore that. You're still mostly human. We can use your powers to make the Hunters more powerful. We can eradicate the werewolves completely. We can even get rid of Cameron. The Human Liaison is always the most powerful and protected, but with your help, we could end their reign for good."

I snap away from him, shock turning into a boiling anger. "Do you hear yourself? What is wrong with you?" I didn't speak too harshly before. I thought I'd known Jack, but I guess I never did. Having a dead mother doesn't excuse genocide.

The softness from his face disappears. In its place lies a cold and unnerving mask. I dart to the other side of his room. He speaks harshly, "I'd think about this before you do anything rash. It could be deadly if you don't agree to help the Hunters."

I force out a laugh. "You think you could defeat the werewolves just because you have weapons? They have supernatural strength. *I* have supernatural strength."

Now, he gives an ugly laugh. Suddenly, all his beauty disappears. He steps closer to me. "You seem very confident in your abilities. I'm sure you don't even understand yet. Hunters are stronger than you think. I mean, look at all those werewolves we killed and left in the clearing."

"You..." I struggle to get the words from my throat. "You killed all those people? You said werewolves were the murderers."

"I didn't want to reveal everything to you yet. You just found out your father was part werewolf. You needed some time to realize how evil they were before I told you more. We had already made it look like animal attacks so the police would think it was their fault. Maybe then they would stop protecting the Human Liaison, but it didn't work. They were just more scared to take any action."

There it is—the truth to the story that brought me here. Days ago, I would have thought the answer to the mystery would bring me closure—this was all I needed to go home. But now, this truth might bring me to my end. Surely, Jack won't let me go home with this knowledge—not that it would be possible to return to my normal life anyway. Cameron's face pops into my brain.

I clear my throat. "We're too powerful for you to kill all of us, even with my help."

He's getting closer to me, pushing me into a corner. "I wish you'd stop lumping yourself in with those bastards. You're different. But no, except Cameron, most werewolves are no match for our years of training. The Human Liaison is always the strongest. Maybe after today, we'll get him, but I doubt it. Sure, we could defeat him with all our manpower and silver chains, but there's an agreement to leave him alone as long as the rest of the humans are safe. That agreement is now broken, not that we cared to keep it intact. He was just the last one on our kill list. They are the only werewolf that discloses their identity publicly to state officials. They keep the peace between humans and Weres. Once one of us finds the identity of a Were, we kill them, but it's not so simple with the Human Liaison. But with you... he obviously seems fond of you and with your powers..."

"Stop! I'm not going to help you! I love him!" I don't know why I say it. Surely, I don't believe it. I just met the guy and hated him literally yesterday, but the words popped out of my mouth without control. My emotions are too all over the place right now. Maybe that's why I'm not speaking rationally. Sure, it's obvious I feel strongly for him, but love? Love is crazy.

He looms over me as my back hits the wall—outstretching his arms on either side of my head. "Love him? We fucked a few days ago." He shakes his head. I don't recognize his face. "I bet you fucked him too, didn't you?" He turns his head away from me as if my smell repulses him. "God, did you move to New York and become a slut?" His eyes turn back to mine, blazing with rage.

My mind turns to survival mode. Right now, I need to stop defending Cameron and the werewolves. I need to get the hell out of here because I'm cornered by the real beast in the woods.

His eyes study mine, darting back and forth as if he's trying to find the best words to slice me. "I'd rather you'd help with your own free will, but if you refuse, we have ways to erase your memories. Just like we did with Granny." He runs a finger down my cheek, and my stomach flips. "It's not pretty and may take years, but we'll get your mind how we want it. We can use you for our cause." He stops—his face morphing as if an idea popped into his head. "With your powers and my influence, we could bring a new generation of Hunters." He has an evil smile. "God, I might just keep Cameron alive long enough so he can witness you carrying my child."

Okay, it's time to freak out. Jack is long past jaded lover and has reached explosive manic levels. Normally, my fight or flight would kick in, and I would choose the latter, but something different boils through me. Red covers my vision, and before I even have a second to think, I grab Jack's throat.

His eyes bulge, and he reaches for my wrist. He claws at my hands, but I don't let up, watching as the panic and shock rises to his eyes. My mind races with what to do next. I hope I can cut his airway off long enough that he passes out. He's an evil man, and I hate him right now, but I don't want to kill him. With all my thoughts, I must release a small amount of pressure.

Jack brings up his knee, hitting me in the stomach. Even with my powers ignited, the surprise attack knocks the air from my body and releases my hold on my strength. I double over.

Jack is too quick, and before I have time to attack again, he hits my chin and knocks my head against the back of the wall. I'm slumped on the ground, my vision tunneling to darkness. So much for wolfy powers.

31

WHEN I NEED YOU MOST

Pain in my head and neck wakes me from my slumber. As I blink my eyes open and slowly register my surroundings, the pounding from the back of my head increases. Jesus Christ, if I make it out of Jack's dungeon, I'll need to see a doctor. From how many times I've been knocked out over the last few days, I should be brain-dead. I pray my werewolf strength can help me withstand injuries, although I'm not confident in my abilities after being overtaken by a man yet again.

I wiggle my hands, tied behind my back to the wooden chair I'm sitting on, and swivel my head, looking for any opportunity to escape. Jack placed my chair in the middle of the room, right under the creepy dangling lightbulb. It's not on, though; the only light comes from the foggy window to my left. I push myself up in the chair to scoot to the workbench. I slam back onto the concrete floor without even moving an inch. It will take forever to reach the other side of the room. By the time I make any progress, Jack will likely be back. Hello? Wolfy strength. Where are you now when I need you most?

I stop struggling for a moment, the pain from my position begging for my attention. "Fuck," I mutter as I let my head drop to my chest. How could I be so stupid? I should have picked up on the signs that Jack was a psychopath. I used to believe no one could be completely evil—they had to have a motive. Even when Jack had me hating the werewolves, a part of me couldn't rationalize hating a whole group. But witnessing Jack's hate toward the Weres changes my mind. Sure, his mother was killed by Weres—so he thinks—but to commit mass murder to such a large group of werewolves—not just Weres, people—evil must surely swim through his veins.

Still, I shouldn't have said I *loved* Cameron when it's not even true. Of course, that would push Jack over the edge. I should have just said whatever I could to get the hell out of Jack's cabin and back to Granny.

Granny. Surely, she's filed a missing person for me by now. At her age, worrying about me can't be good for her health, but maybe Jack's told her some sort of lie to keep her off the case. My mind races with horrible images of the torture Granny must have endured to forget about my family's lineage. Why would they want her to forget her Hunter history and that her son-in-law was a werewolf? I guess she'd grown to love my father, but the Hunters didn't want her to grow soft.

No, that's not it. How could I be so stupid?

Werewolves didn't murder my parents. The Hunters did.

A sob escapes from the back of my throat. I'd been so shocked to hear that the Hunters were the ones to kill all those people that I didn't put the pieces together to realize that if the Hunters were so set on eradicating werewolves, obviously, my dad would be on their kill list. Even if my dad was the Human Liaison and the most powerful, they still could have killed him. My parents would never have agreed to help the Hunters. I don't need anyone to confirm it—I just know they wouldn't, even if I didn't know them very well.

The sorrow quickly turns to anger. I struggle against my binds again. I don't just need to get out of here not to be tortured and impregnated; I need to avenge my parents.

My newfound rage ignites my strength, and I jump my chair closer to the workbench. A shiny pair of pliers catch my attention. Jack's an idiot to leave them out, but obviously, he doesn't think I'm capable of much. Sweat drips down my forehead as I get closer and closer, and my heart pounds in my chest, anticipating Jack barging through the door at any moment. One last jump until I reach the pliers. I use all my strength but overcompensate, crashing to the floor on my side. "Fuck," I mutter as a new wave of pain spreads down the side of my body. I wait for Jack to rush in—already anticipating his smug remarks about how I failed miserably to escape.

A crash comes from above. I dart my attention to the window, closing my eyes as glass breaks and falls to the workbench above me.

"Red," a worried voice whispers into the room.

"Cameron!" I yell, nearly sobbing.

He pulls himself through the window, ignoring the broken glass around him. He jumps quietly to the floor beside me and pulls my chair upright. "That fucking prick," he mutters before leaning over and snapping the zip-ties around my wrists with his teeth.

I gasp in relief as I yank my hands in front of me, rubbing at the red sores. "How did you know to find me here?"

He kneels in front of me, desperation painted on his face as he grasps my hands in his. He brings my wrists up to his lips, kissing them hungrily. "The Hunters—I smelled them coming before they arrived. I had a key in my pocket and freed myself before they got to me. You were gone," he says in a pained voice in between his kisses. "I looked for you. I felt it in my bones that something was wrong. I knew you wouldn't have escaped after last night."

Tears of relief well in my eyes. I look down at him—his dark hair tousled, his face back to clean-shaven—the sight of him stirs something in me. I don't wrestle with the thoughts about how I just went from one man's prisoner to the next. He's right. I wasn't a prisoner after last night. Something changed inside of me, even if I can't explain it.

He sits on his knees, noticing my eyes taking him in, reaching out and pulling me to his lips. He kisses me desperately, yanking the air from my lungs. "I thought I'd lost you," he says between a hurried breath, his voice needy and his hands running up my legs.

God, his touch melts me in place. I'd love to let him take me here and have Jack walk in to witness it. The idea sparks a bit of rationale in my mind. *Jack.* We're in his house, and he could be back any second. In fact, we're extremely lucky he hasn't already barged in here. He must have left to speak to the other Hunters to tell them about me.

I push him away. "Cameron, we have to go."

He shakes his head. "Yeah, of course." He stands and extends his hand.

I rise, the floor unsteady under my feet, and I cling to him. He wraps his arms around me. "Are you okay?"

"Yeah." I nod, clenching my eyes and willing the pain in my head to leave. I want to tell him the details of my capture, and that I should probably head to the ER to get an MRI, but from the look on his face—if I showed even an ounce more discomfort, he'd insist we stay and burn the place to the ground.

"Is there somewhere we can go? Somewhere he wouldn't know about? I need to rest and regroup before we deal with all this."

He pulls me into his chest. "I know a place."

I soak in his smell for a moment. Days before, it infuriated me how strong it was. Now, it's like a warm blanket, instantly easing the pain in my head. Maybe I need to spend a few days curled up with him. I don't want to think about what all of this means or what my next steps are to avenge my parents' murders; I just want to smell this man.

Fuck, I'm officially a full-blown animal.

32

MOUNT ME

"**I**'m not getting on your back," I say as I cross my arms over my chest.

"You can barely walk. How do you expect to get five miles from here before the Hunters find us?"

It was a sorry sight to see me climbing out of the window and running far enough away from Jack's cabin for us to re-group. I'm barefoot, and the loungewear Cameron loaned me the day before doesn't do much to protect my bits from the elements. Not to mention my pounding headache. Still, riding on the back of my new werewolf lover—or whatever the hell Cameron is to me—is the last thing I want to do. "Can't we just get your truck?" Although walking back to his cabin makes my feet want to cry, it beats the alternative.

"There are Hunters all over the place. It's too risky."

I twist my lips, wracking my brain for another solution.

Cameron runs his fingers through his hair, sighing. "We don't have time. Stop whining, and let's go," he says in an irritated tone.

Ah, there's the impatient dick I loved so much. I had wondered if his grating personality totally disappeared when he became so obviously fond of me. I can't say the roughness of his tone doesn't send a rush down my spine. I'd love for him to order me around like this in the bedroom. *Fuck, Red. Get yourself together.* I shake my head. "Fine."

It happens so fast that I don't even register when his skin becomes fur, and his teeth become fangs. His clothes fall to the floor beside his new form. Where a man stood now is a wolf, but much larger with black course hair, glowing amber eyes, and pure white fangs. It's the beast from my dream nights ago. I'm sure of it.

I can't unfreeze myself. I dropped to my knees before him when he was halfway transformed, but seeing him entirely in his werewolf form makes it hard to breathe. I'm not terrified, but something chilling runs through my veins.

He approaches me, nudging my hand with his snout before turning and looking back at me.

"Oh, right. I'm supposed to mount you." This is so fucking weird.

I gingerly walk to his side, picking up the pile of clothes next to him. "Do you want me to bring these?" I ask.

He nods.

I grab them and stick them under my armpit before jumping up and grunting as I throw my leg over. He barely gives me a second to brace myself before he takes off. I yelp and cling to his fur, leaning over and pressing my body against him to stay on. He vibrates like he's chuckling.

Trees whip past us, and the wind tears at my clothing. I'm no speedometer, but I swear we're going at least seventy miles per hour. I abandon my efforts to gather where we're going, clenching my eyes shut and burying my face into Cameron's fur. Just when I'm sure I'll have to spend the next hour cleaning vomit off him, he slows, but I don't sit up until he stops.

"Let's never do that again, okay?" I say as I climb down, wobbling once I reach my feet.

The shift happens again, and before I can blink, he's standing at my side, human, naked, and grabbing my arm to steady me. I gaze up at him, awestruck. "That was a fast change," I manage to say.

He chuckles. "Yeah, I'm pretty fast when it's not the Blood Moon, but I like to take my time with most things." His eyes heat over his cocky grin.

"Oh, geez." I push his clothes into his chest, grinning as the blood rushes to my cheeks and trying not to let my eyes trail any lower.

The minute I'm away from his touch, the pain in my head returns. The reality of the last twenty-four hours crashes around me. It's crazy that a few light-hearted moments with Cameron can make me forget everything, but I can't say I hate it.

I rub at my temple.

"Are you okay?" he asks, all humor lost from his voice as he rushes to my side.

"Yeah, I'm fine." The pain instantly melts once he touches me. Okay, I don't think this is in my head anymore. "Why do I feel better when you touch me?"

He smiles and holds my arm to steady himself as he hops into his pants. "What can I say? I have that effect on women?"

"Asshole." The comment should give me the major ick, but I can't help but smile. "But no, really."

"It's part of this whole werewolf thing." His face tenses as if he's holding something back as he buttons up his shirt.

I study him for a moment. "Whatever. Where are we?" I swivel my attention at the canopy of trees overhead.

Cameron takes a deep breath and looks around him, a proud smile forming. "I found this place when I was a teenager. Here, follow me." He grabs my hand, pulling me deeper into the woods, pushing away the brush, and leading me into a clearing.

I don't let go of his hand as I stare, mouth wide, at the sight before me. A crystal blue spring, surrounded by rocks and what looks like a cave, sits in the middle of the area. "Wow."

"I know, right? It's my best-kept secret. I'm sure others know about this place, but I've never seen anyone else here, and it's not on any maps. We can sleep in the cave tonight."

Sleeping. With Cameron. Tonight.

My body transforms into some hormonal teenage boy. Cameron can't even mention plans for our shelter without my mind jumping to images of me fucking him. God, being a werewolf blows. Literally. I hope I don't spend time with other werewolf men in case I'm this feral around all of them.

Cameron jumps to the edge of the spring, balancing on one foot to the next as he walks closer to the cave's entrance. "Come on, let me show you the place." He looks so boyish, so full of joy. Nothing like the man I met in the woods who called me an idiot and reeked of danger. My cheeks hurt from smiling as I follow after him, keeping my feet on solid ground instead of the rocky barrier Cameron follows since I'm probably recovering from a concussion.

My eyes adjust to the darkness as I duck inside the cave. Cameron grabs a sleeping bag and pillows rolled up against the wall and shakes out the dust.

"Is this where you usually bring your flings?" I ask, resting against the wall as I watch him.

"Is that what you think you are? A fling?" He doesn't take his eyes off the sleeping bag as he rolls it out on the floor.

My cheeks heat. I'm unsure if he means I'm less than that or more. I can't help my heart hoping for the latter. Stupid heart.

I sit, crossing my legs, trying to ignore my pounding organs. "Well, what am I to you, Cameron? I used to think I was your next meal, but…"

"Used to? Oh, don't give up that notion." He lifts his stare to me, his eyes heated.

I blush, grinning and turning away from him. "Shut up."

"Is that what you want? I can be quiet, although I love to make noise."

I give an incredulous laugh. "You're relentless, aren't you."

He gets up on all fours. "When it comes to my prey, yes."

I lift myself, ready to jump to my feet. "Is that what I am to you, prey?" I crawl backward.

"You look like it right now." The pheromones drip from his being. The smell of him envelopes me.

We both freeze, waiting for each other's next movement. The air is thick with the sexual tension between us. All this flirting has made me forget everything, and I want it to stay that way for a little while longer. Scratch that; I want it to go *past* that. I want to see just how far Cameron will take this predator and prey game.

I jump to my feet, rushing out of the cave and toward the spring, adrenaline ridding my body of all its aches and pains.

He's right behind me, and I fight myself from turning back to see what forms he's taken to chase me. His hot breath tickles my neck, but just before he reaches me, I jump into the water, and he follows me in. I swim away, but it's useless; his arms wrap around me, turning me to him and pulling me up to the surface.

I gulp in air, my screams and laughter bursting from me. I push at him, using all my might to swim away, even as I revel in the feeling of his muscles constricting around me.

"Let me go!" I yell, still smiling and giggling like a schoolgirl.

"No," he says as he grabs my legs, wrapping them around his waist.

My skin prickles as his erection presses against my core, and I pick up my gaze, meeting his ravenous stare. The game is over. My heart hammers out of my chest, and my lips part—the air suddenly too heavy for my lungs.

Cameron raises his hand, tucking a loose, wet hair behind my ear. My eyes close, and I lean into him.

"You asked what you are to me."

His words stop my journey to his lips, and my eyes burst open. "What?" I whisper.

"You're my mate."

The clouds around this moment disappear, and I scrunch my face in confusion. "What?"

"That's what you are to me. You're my everything. You're my mate. Do you know what that means?"

I know what that means. I know what it means more than I know anything, and from what my body is screaming at me, the word just made the mess of my life a hell of a lot messier.

Oh fuck.

33

NEVER ENOUGH

I push him away. "Stop."

Hurt floods his eyes as he reaches for me, but I swim around him, making my way to shore.

"Red, I can't help it."

"I don't want to hear it. I can't deal with this right now." It's all too much. I just found out I have were-wolf powers, my childhood best friend and brief lover is a psychopath, and my parents were murdered by a group of people I share ancestry with. My life is in danger. Now isn't the time to fling myself into a lifelong romance. I'm not sure of the specifics of what he claims between us, but it's like some ancient and powerful part of me beats in my chest, telling me everything I need to know. It's too much—too much for a girl like me who plans to return to New York if I ever make it out of here alive. Seconds ago, a part of me hoped I could be more to him than just a fling, but I can tell *this* is much more than anything I had in mind.

He grabs my arm, twisting me toward him. "Do you even understand what I'm saying to you?" His fingers tighten around my forearms, and his mouth hardens into a line. Fire and fury blaze behind his eyes.

I match his expression, furious that he could possibly be angry with me right now. "No, and I don't want to know!"

He pulls me closer to him, staring me down and pressing me against his chest. "Why don't you want to know?"

"I just..." I look away from him, tears clouding my vision.

He grabs my chin, yanking my attention to him. "No, tell me. Tell me what you feel."

"It's too much, Cameron. I feel too much." My tears escape.

"No, it's not enough. It will never be enough." He crashes his lips into mine, grabbing the back of my head and keeping me in place.

I don't give in at first, keeping my body rigid, but that spark—that damn spark, and the smell of him, and the taste of him. I melt with a sigh, opening up and letting his tongue explore the inside of my mouth. My hands roam over his chest, covered by his wet T-shirt, even if he doesn't give me room to feel for much.

It's barely been a few seconds of our embrace before he pulls away, crouching down and swinging me into his arms. The second away from his lips is too much, and I wrap my arms around his neck, pulling him to me again as he walks us away from the spring and toward the cave.

He kneels, placing me on the sleeping bag. I sit on my elbows, watching him rip his T-shirt off. His muscles line his entire chest, darkened by the shadows, and trail into a V above the waistline of his jeans. I run my tongue along my lip, the anticipation of the taste of him killing me.

"Take your clothes off." His voice startles me back to the moment.

I contemplate for a second. Should I be a brat and put up a fight? Or should I do what he says to get my bare skin against him sooner? Apparently, the contemplation is too much. He falls over me, holding himself up with his outstretched arms. "Did you hear me, mate? I said take off your clothes, or I'll swallow you whole."

I furrow my brow. "I'm not your mate." Even as I say it, my body welcomes him, my breath heavies, and I puff out my chest.

"Do you need me to show you? My knot, it's only there for you."

The mention of his knot makes my mouth water. I unbuckle his pants and reach down his underwear to feel him, keeping my eyes glued to his.

"Fuck," he mutters before clenching his eyes and letting his head fall to his chest as I fit my fingers around him, stroking him down until I reach his base, stopping there to feel that part of him—that part that will tie me to him. My mind races with what it will feel like to have them fully hardened inside of me, sealing his come inside of me—making me his.

"Do you know what this means? If we do this, there's no turning back."

"Do I have a choice?"

"Do you have a choice, Red? Fuck. Yes, you have a choice." He pushes himself away from me, and my hand slips from him, but he doesn't lose my gaze. "My primal instinct wants to take you regardless, but I'm stronger than that. I know you feel this, too, and I'm tired of you hiding from it. I'm tired of you acting like you don't want to be locked in my bedroom or you don't want to be bound to me forever. I'll push you to your edge, but if you don't want this—I stop. Fate might have decided we are destined for each other, but you still have a say. Say the word, and I'll stop."

My eyes tear again. Maybe I wasn't terrified of the connection between Cameron and me. Maybe I knew since the moment I laid eyes on him that it was him and no one else, regardless of how hard I tried to ignore it. Maybe the real part that terrifies me is the choice. When I hear the word mate, it means life partners—predestined and unquestionable.

"Is this what you want?" I ask. "Me? Or is it just what your body says you need?" I ask for an answer from him as much as I ask myself.

He lowers himself again, millimeters away from my lips. "I want all of you, Red. I want your fire, your sarcasm, your drive. You're a pain in the ass, but I've always enjoyed pain. I'll admit, I don't know you as much as I'd like to, but I have forever to figure you out. No part of me wishes you were different."

His words melt into my pores, turning me from the inside out. I meet his lips with mine, yanking his body closer to me. I pull away and bring my lips to his ears. "I want this. I'm done fighting it."

It's as if my words flipped a switch, turning man into animal. His kisses deepen, and his hands stretch my tank top until it tears down the middle, and he pushes it away—exposing my breasts. He reaches for me, palming one breast—my nipples pebbling. He moans and moves down my body to suck on the other. "Your skin—I need to lick all of you."

Every word, every touch—my veins thicken, and the blood that flows inside heats. Power radiates from my fingertips. Too many feelings assault my nerve endings: the lust, the power, the need. I'm on the brink of something great, and the anticipation rushes through me like electricity.

I tug at his hair as his licks roam lower down my body, peppering kisses on my stomach. When he reaches my shorts, he grabs the bottom, tugging them off my body. His mouth hovers over my seam, and he breathes me in. "God, Red, your scent. It's fucking intoxicating. I might come just from the scent of you."

And I might just come from that sentence, but I will myself to hold off. I need to feel all of him. I need him inside of me—filling me and making me his.

His tongue dances down my cunt, teasing me as if he's savoring his meal. I buck against him, needing the friction. He applies more pressure, pushing his tongue inside me and lapping slowly. I cry, the pleasure swirling around in bright colors behind my eyelids.

He picks up his head, and I gasp from the loss of contact. "I've never been a religious man, but God, could I worship every inch of you."

His words entice another moan from me. "God, just fuck me already." I cry, loving the way he's enjoying me but urgently needing my release.

"Not yet. I'm taking my time with you. I've waited my whole life for my mate." He brings his head back down to my cunt, pushing my legs wide and swirling his tongue through me. He takes long, slow, delicious licks, but I need more. I grind against him, urging him to my clit. His fingers tightened on my hip bones, and he pushed me down. Power surges through me, and I know that I could overcome his strength if I used all my might, but even though my body begs for more, I can't deny that I would love his desire to ring me out until I'm desperate.

"Cameron, please," I cry, tugging at his hair to emphasize my point.

I feel his grin against my cunt as he shakes his head slightly. He focuses his attention on my clit, swirling his tongue around the sensitive bud. He inserts a finger inside of me, fucking me with his hand in tempo with his strokes.

It doesn't take long before I'm barreling toward my orgasm, the walls of my pussy clenching around his fingers. "Oh, God." I cry out. He barely waits a second before he crawls up my body, his scruff scrapping below my ear. "I'm your God now. I only want to hear my name on your lips."

I grin, turning my head to face him. "Well, Lord and Savior, please, for the love of Cameron, fuck me already."

This time, the smile against my neck holds more point. He scrapes his fangs down my neck, and the slight pain pulls a cry of pleasure from me. I wrap my legs around him, and his dick slides through my wetness. My body begs for release again as if my orgasm didn't even happen. I angle my hips, urging him to thrust inside of me.

His tip meets me, and he stops, his body shuddering. "I don't want to hurt you," he says as if the hesitation is killing him.

I bite down on his neck, my teeth sinking into his skin. When I pull away, I notice the marks. My teeth have turned into fangs. Cameron cries out, and I whisper into his ear. "You're not the only one who enjoys pain."

That's all he needs. He pounds into me—so forcefully that it rattles my skull. "Fuck," I yell, holding onto him as his thrusts deepen.

"This won't last long," he says between labored breaths.

It won't last long for me either. The feel of his cock hitting the back of me—filling me, throbbing with the need to release—it's all too much. This knot stretches me out at my opening. There's pain in the stretching, but it's so deliciously good that I can't help but wish for more—anticipating the feel of his knot fully hardened inside of me. "Cameron, my God," I yell, throwing my head back.

"That's right, my mate. I am your god, and you are mine."

My body clenches around him. Heat explodes from the back of my eyes, and my mind focuses. I gasp, the feeling of my orgasm doubles. Cameron cries out, and his warmness coats the inside of me. I feel it. Not just what it's doing to me, but I feel it from his perspective. "Cameron!" I cry, barely able to get the words out, on the brink of passing out from so much pleasure. "I feel you. I feel what you feel." His knot swells, growing inside and gluing him to me. The pain heightens, and for good measure, I tug against him just to see what will happen. I barely move an inch. We're completely connected. I pull him closer, running my hands down his back, reveling in the feeling. I've never felt so full, so complete, so wanted.

Cameron's head rests at my side as he gathers his breath. He finally rises to his elbows to loom over me, shock riddled across his face.

"What?" I ask with a smile. Nothing could damper my mood at this moment.

He studies me, his eyes darting over mine. "Red, your eyes. They're glowing."

34

ENDGAME

I watch as the light dims from my eyes on the selfie camera of Cameron's phone before the battery dies completely. "Why is this happening?" I ask, turning back to Cameron, lying on his side next to me. He's already placed our wet clothes on stones outside the cave to dry. He's completely naked, wrapped in part of the sleeping bag, with his head propped up by a muscular arm as he rests a hand on my thigh. "I've heard about powerful werewolves who had the power of mind reading. Their eyes glow whenever they use their abilities. I've just never met one in real life."

I shoot him a disbelieving look before tossing the phone to him. "Are you fucking with me?" I lie down next to him, and he pulls me in close. I hide my sharp breath as I revel in the feel of his muscular body pushed against mine.

He grins and kisses my cheek, his hand running lazily up and down my bare back. "No, I'm being serious. I think coming together with me—your mate—is helping you transition into your full powers." He looks me in the eyes and shakes his head slightly. "And damn, are you powerful."

"I wonder what else I can do." My mind replays the feelings—Cameron's feelings—my cunt pulsing around him. Having two orgasms barrel through me at once was the most mind-fucking, amazing experience I've ever had, but that can't be the purpose of my powers. I'm not a very powerful werewolf if I can only read minds during sex.

"We'll have to start training so you can reach your full potential."

My fingers travel up and down his back, feeling the subtle remnants of the scratches I caused nights before. They should be worse, but I guess his werewolf powers offer some sort of healing effect. "Sorry about these."

He grabs my arm and brings my fingers to his lips to kiss. "Are you kidding me? I'm hard just thinking about you scratching the shit out of me." He nudges into me slightly as if he needs his erection to prove the point. "It's every male's dream to help their mate come into their full power. I never would have dreamed mine would be so powerful."

"So that wasn't because of the Blood Moon? It was because of you?" I mentally scan my body, noticing that the pain in my head and feet is almost gone.

"The Blood Moon probably had a little to do with it, but you can thank me for your sudden burst of strength and all-around euphoric feeling." He smirks.

I shove his shoulder with a grin. "Okay, cocky asshole."

He wraps his arms tighter around me and kisses up my neck. "I'm sorry, I will never compare to my powerful mate. I'm a jealous prick."

"I thought you were the most powerful werewolf."

He pulls me back to study me. "Who told you that?"

"Jack." Nerves shoot up my spine. I hate that I must bring him into this moment, and I'm nervous Cameron will become all macho alpha jealous.

He laughs, his smile reaching his brown eyes. "Seems a bit odd of him to mention that about the competition, but hey, I guess I should thank him for the compliment."

I shove him. "Hey, he's not competition!"

He cups my chin. "Oh, believe me, *I know.* I doubt he sees it that way. But honestly, what a weird thing to say."

I giggle a little. "Yeah, you should have seen him. He did the whole, "I'm going to reveal my evil plan before the good guy comes and saves the day" shit. So very stereotypical evil villain." Jack's more complex than that. He's grown up thinking werewolves murdered both of our parents. He's been brainwashed, but there comes a point when adults must decide for themselves between good and evil, and he clearly made the wrong choice.

Cameron shakes his head before resting it in the crook of my neck. "And they say werewolves have dog-sized brains." He takes a big breath, inhaling the smell of me. I guess being obsessed with each other's smell is a werewolf thing, too. "Ah, my mate. We are going to have such powerful kids."

My body stiffens, and panic rings through me. Obviously, the whole knot thing is to ensure I get pregnant, but during sex, the idea was hot. Maybe I've always had a breeding kink, but now reality has settled around me. Breeding means babies. Babies mean a whole new life. I've given myself over to Cameron. He's my mate, and coming together with him completely made my body's reaction to him fully connect in my brain. He's endgame for me. But there's so much we haven't figured out. Are we going to live here together? Get married? Push out a litter of pups right away? I have a life in New York—friends. Am I ready to give that up and settle down here?

"Woah, woah, woah." Cameron grabs my neck, sensing my internal panic and urging my darting eyes to focus on his. "Stop freaking out. You don't get pregnant until you're ready."

"But Cameron, we just... You just..."

"I know what it feels like, but I'm basically shooting blanks until you're ready."

"What?" Is he on... birth control?

He sighs. "I'm sorry, I forget how little you know about us. It's a werewolf thing. Females can't get pregnant until they want to. Your brain controls your body. Female werewolves have amazing mental abilities. It's kind of a version of the mind reading."

I exhale, feeling the weight of the world thin around me. I'm not fully a werewolf, not even close, but I do apparently have mind-reading powers, so I imagine I can have the power not to get pregnant.

Cameron wraps me in an embrace. "We've got a lot to figure out before we start thinking about kids. Although, I can't say my primitive male brain doesn't revel in the idea."

I smile. "I wish I knew you when you were a kid."

"Yeah, I have a feeling life would have been much easier if you were around." A heaviness clouds his eyes.

I draw circles down his arms. "What was it like—your childhood?"

"Pretty lonely. Werewolf identities are top secret since we must hide from the Hunters. My identity has been known since I was a kid. My powers came early, so everyone knew I'd be the Human Liaison one day.

None of the other werewolf kids could hang out with me. It was just Carmen and me."

"What about your parents?"

"Dead. Hunters." He shrugs as if it's a typical thing.

Sadness fills me. Even though my parents fell to the same fate, it seems worse that Cameron had to experience growing up as an orphan. Maybe that's what happens when you have a mate—their sadness supersedes your own.

"Who took care of you?"

"We got tossed around to different council members. Old werewolves that were never at too great of a risk."

"Did you go to school?" More questions bubble at the surface of my brain. There's his whole life I need to know about.

"Yeah, we went to McKlenny, but we weren't allowed to get too close to any children. We were a walking hazard."

"Oh! We used to play McKlenny in sports! I went to Howard."

"Yeah, I know." He smiles.

"How do you know?"

"I knew who you were, Red, remember? I always knew you as Mildred, so it took me a while to put together."

I cringe at my name. "Oh, yeah. That's right." When he told me he knew my father earlier, I didn't put together that it meant he knew of me growing up.

"I could sense you were my mate the moment I saw you in that clearing. It infuriated me. You were a New York Times reporter, threatening to reveal my people's identity, plus the Blood Moon made me extra irritable."

"I could tell." I scoff.

He cups my face, smiling. "I'm sorry, okay? I was an idiot." His smile melts a bit. "Anyways, your father took me under his wing when I was six and you were four. He was always talking about you."

"Really? What would he say?" A piece of my father. I hadn't realized how desperate I was to hear more about him.

"He just talked about how smart and talented you were. You were always getting in trouble in school, just like your mom used to. He would tell me that someday he'd bring you by the Council meetings so

I could meet you, but that day never came." His eyes fill with sadness.

I nod. "I wish I would have known you. I didn't have many friends either. Especially in high school." I don't bother mentioning Jack was my only friend. There's no need to bring him up in this conversation twice.

He shakes his head. "I always knew Howard was full of a bunch of idiots."

I chuckle and hit his arm. "Hey! I went there, remember?"

"Oh, you were the exception, my mate—absolutely."

I kiss him with a smile, my toes curling. I gaze into his eyes, not wanting the conversation to end. I want to share everything about my childhood with him. I want to know everything about him.

"You wouldn't have liked me in high school. I was chubby." I immediately regret my words. What the fuck is he supposed to say to that? Now I'm just word vomiting.

His head jerks back. "What? I know what you looked like in high school; you were fucking sexy."

I roll my eyes, even if my heart lifts over the fact that he kept tabs on me all these years until I left for New York. "Okay, shut up. That was a stupid thing of me to bring up. I wasn't asking you to lie to me about being skinny."

He grabs my chin. "I said you were fucking sexy, not skinny. Your size doesn't make you any less or more beautiful."

My heart hammers in my chest. His words. My childhood self heals a little. A tear rolls down my cheek. He wipes it away. I should have dealt with my body issues years ago, but I always kept myself too busy. Of course, I need to learn to love myself at any size, but to know I have a partner—a mate—who loves me in all my forms, does make the work less daunting.

I tether my lips to him, wrapping my arms around his neck and pulling him into me. My core heats, and I grind against him. I swear this man could get me off just by his words. His hands explore my backside, picking up my ass and grinding me against his length. I'm about to climb on, fuck him again until I can't see straight, but then he pulls back. "Red, before we start again—because I want to fuck you fully and thoroughly, we should talk about our next move."

It takes a second for my brain to settle, but I nod and gulp. "Yeah, you're right." I sit up to look outside the cave entrance. It's nearly nighttime. We've spent a whole day hiding out. "Granny. We need to get back to her and make sure she's okay." I start to stand, but Cameron pulls me back. "It's not safe, Red. You still need time to heal, and it's too dangerous to do so in the middle of the night."

I pull away. "I feel fine."

"That's just because you're close to me. The mating bond has healing effects. You need to rest for a night with me before we go and battle the Hunters. Granny will be fine. She's a civilian. If the Hunters mess with her, they face a whole sleuth of legal repercussions."

"They didn't seem to care about legal repercussions when Jack kidnapped me and tied me to a chair." I don't mention that he also threatened to torture and impregnate me. Although I hate to admit it, Cameron's right about me needing time to heal, and if I mention that, he'll go full monster mode, and I do need a whole night snuggling up to him. But I sure as hell won't be able to get any sleep without knowing I thought of every possible option to go to Granny first.

"You're part werewolf, remember? They are well aware of your family's lineage. The police force couldn't care less about us. Unless the Human Liaison is hurt."

"So Hunters can just kill dozens of werewolves without any repercussion?"

"No. They'll still pay attention to mass murder. We just haven't been able to prove that the people killed and placed in that clearing were killed by Hunters. The police think it's a few rouge werewolves."

"I can vouch. Jack told me everything. If they don't listen to me, I'll threaten to leak a story."

Cameron nods. "That's what I'm hoping. We'll check on Granny in the morning, and then visit Sergeant Brick. Threaten him to treat the murders seriously, or you'll exploit the corruption.

"I'll need more evidence, though."

Silence passes between us before the idea pops into my head. "I'll need to record Jack's confession. If he revealed everything before, he'll do it again."

"No."

"But Cameron..."

"No! I'm not leaving you with that psychopath again!" His voice raises, and the veins in his neck bulge.

I grab his arm, letting him feel my power as my grip tightens. "I don't need protecting. Once I regain my strength, I can protect myself." I say it to convince myself as much as him. He's overpowered me once, but now I know a fraction more about my capabilities. I just need a full night's rest, and I could beat him.

He sighs, reaching for me. I allow him to pull me close and lie down next to him. "I know, but there has to be a better way."

"I'm listening."

His fangs prick my neck. "Cameron!" It still amazes me that he can transform parts of himself so quickly.

"Maybe I was wrong to prolong fucking to figure this out. I think I need to fill you up again so my brain can work at full capacity." His hand reaches for my breasts, and his erection presses against my ass.

I exhale. "Cameron," I say in a warning tone, even if my body betrays me and I lean into him.

"Okay, okay, fine. We'll do it your way. Just fuck me already."

I laugh as his fingers find the heat pooling between my legs, and I sigh in satisfaction. And just like that, my worries for the morning dissipate from my brain.

35

SILVER CHAINS

Okay, maybe riding on the back of a werewolf isn't that bad when you know he's your mate. Something about the whole predestined, only-for-each-other sentiment makes it a little less degrading and a hell of a lot more arousing.

We woke at the crack of dawn. I could barely believe how much better I felt after a full night's sleep and a few orgasms with my mate. I feel better than I have in years, which gives me the confidence that I'll be able to defeat Jack and the Hunters.

The plan is to check on Granny, fill her in on everything that's happened, and hope she's not too brainwashed to ignore it or suffer another seizure. Cameron will stay with her to ensure her safety. I will head to Jack's, mustering up all my high-school theater kid skills to put on the biggest performance of my life and act like Cameron did, in fact, brainwash me, and now I am back to myself and want to help Jack defeat the werewolves—all while recording the conversation and getting him to reveal that the Hunters murdered those people in the clearing. Jack may be stupid, but I doubt he'll believe it. I hope a little cleavage and stroking his ego will do the trick. If anything, he'll tie me up and reveal his evil plan like a nineteen-fifties cartoon villain like he did last time. Hopefully, I don't get knocked out again, but I'm not too worried since I know I have a mate with a powerful, all-healing dick.

We couldn't get Cameron's truck to drive to Granny's—too much of a risk, and although I tried to insist that I could make the journey on my own two feet, it didn't take Cameron much to convince me to hop on his wolfy back. It would take forever by human feet.

My fingers dig into his coarse fur, Cameron's folded clothes wedged between my armpit, and I hunch forward as he sprints through the woods. My cunt grinds up and down on his back, and I nearly get off from the sensation. I'm not focused on the alarming speed or keeping the granola bar Cameron gave me before we left in my stomach. The sensation of his body under mine holds all of my attention.

I bite back a moan as Cameron slows down near the winding driveway to Granny's house. I clench my eyes and focus on returning my breathing to a normal tempo as I climb off Cameron, doing my best to think of un-arousing things—baseball, taxes—fuck it's hard.

"Are you okay?" Cameron asks, already transformed into his human form, completely naked. He takes my hand, and I will myself to focus on his eyes.

My cheeks heat, and I hand him his clothes from under my armpit. "Yeah, it's just..." I search for the right words.

He chuckles, stepping into his underwear. My eyes dart to his large dick before they disappear underneath the fabric. "Don't worry, feeling your wet cunt pressed against me was hot as fuck for me too." He hops in his pants and pulls his shirt over his muscular torso before pulling me in and kissing me.

I surrender myself to him, leaning in as his hands explore my backside. Thankfully, we're hidden by bushes at the side of Granny's yard. I grind against his length, hard under his jeans. The kiss deepens, and I'm about to completely drift away into a land of euphoria when a rational thought pops into my brain—we're not here to fuck in Granny's yard.

I pull back. "We should probably check on Granny," I say, breathy and labored.

He clenches his eyes and nods. "Yeah. You're right." He blows out a breath and adjusts himself before straightening his shoulders. "Alright, let's go." He grabs my hand and walks toward Granny's house.

The front door is unlocked as usual, and I swing it open. She only locks things up at night. "Granny, I'm home!" I call as I enter. I don't hear anything at first. Maybe she's sleeping. Her Volkswagon is out front, so I know she must be home. "Granny!" I try again, Cameron at my heels as I walk into the living room.

A sound comes from the kitchen, and my heart beats faster. I look back toward Cameron before charging toward the source. "Granny!" I scream once my eyes meet my Grandmother; her eyes are closed, but her chest rises and falls—sitting in a dining room chair—her hands bound behind her back.

Jack steps out from a shadow and places his hand on Granny's shoulder—his other hand puts a dagger at her throat. His eyes point to two wooden chairs back to back—handcuffs placed on the seat. "Silver chains on—now!"

36

GURGLED SCREAMS

I'm only one-fourth werewolf. You'd think that silver chains would barely affect me. My mind races, remembering if I ever wore silver jewelry growing up. Now that I think of it, I'd always been more of a gold girl. I probably wouldn't have noticed silver affecting me before since I hadn't come into my powers. As I yank at the silver handcuff securing my hands behind the wooden chair, it's obvious my powers have dissipated from me. Cameron remains still, confirming that he doesn't doubt the effectiveness of the chains. I'm able to reach the power button on the top of the recorder in my back pocket, just in case I make it out of here.

Jack paces back and forth to our side, his hands running through his auburn hair. "It shouldn't have turned out this way," he mumbles to himself. "You were supposed to be with me. You're barely a werewolf." He turns to me now, his face red.

I can't take my eyes off him as if something on his person will reveal how it's possible that the man I loved for most of my life could turn out to be so evil. My mind replays moments from high school. He had his jealous moments. He never liked me hanging out with others but would ignore me in a group setting. It's like he always wanted to keep me to himself. I went from thinking he never felt the same way about me—to thinking he cared about my future—to now, I don't know what.

"My father told me we would get married one day. He even made sure Granny was rewired to enforce this narrative. Do you know how hard it is growing up with your parents telling you who you need to love?"

I dart my attention to Granny, still breathing but unconscious in her binds. My eyes well with tears as I think of all she had to endure over the years. I could have ended all of it. I could have avenged her and my parents, but now I'm tied to a chair—useless.

He doesn't wait for me to answer. "You were so fond of me, and I felt like something was wrong with me for not feeling the same way. I told you I loved you at graduation because my father made me. He thought it would make you stay."

"So you never loved me?" I don't care anymore, but I'd like to get my facts straight.

He stops walking and turns to me. "I cared for you, Red, I did, but not in the same way—not like my father wanted me to. Then you had to cause that earthquake, and everyone suspected you might have powers, so they blamed me for letting you go."

I smack my lips and roll my eyes. "Great. I'm glad that's settled. Then just let us go." Did he ever really punch Todd Silvers for talking bad about me? I want to ask, but it seems pointless now.

He charges toward me, and Cameron jerks in his seat. Jack stops, sizing Cameron up and down as Cameron snarls up at him. Jack speaks, not taking his eyes off Cameron. "But then you came back, and you were different. I fell for you the way my father always wanted me to. I finally saw what we were meant to be—to bring in the new generation of Hunters—to eradicate the werewolves. But then you had to whore around and sleep with the enemy days after letting me fuck you."

"Watch it!" Cameron yells.

Jack leans in his face. "I know you used werewolf mind powers on her. There's no way she would sleep with you in her right mind."

Cameron spits on Jack's face.

Jack stands, gathering his composure before punching Cameron across the jaw.

"Stop!" I yell, tears falling down my cheek. "He's my mate!"

Jack turns to me. "Your what?"

I don't reply—regret churning in my gut that I revealed too much.

Cameron's fingers find mine from behind my back, and he holds onto me.

Jack laughs, returning to his pacing. "Is that what he told you? Your mate. That's a load of shit. You might have discovered some *special abilities* inherited by your bastard of a father, but you're mostly human. You can't overpower me, and you can't have a mate. God, think for yourself, Red."

I don't even contemplate his words. I know what I feel, and it's real, but maybe it's better if he thinks of me as weak—mostly human. Maybe that's our ticket out of this.

"Cameron's always been jealous of me. Growing up, my father had me keep an eye on him. I was so much more powerful than you when we were kids. I never tired of putting you in your place whenever I saw you in town. But then you got older, grew into your powers, and had so much protection. Did you think you would get revenge on me by stealing my girl?"

Cameron sighs. "You think too highly of yourself. You never crossed my mind."

Jack gives a pained laugh. "I'm sure. You fucking Human Liaisons think you're so tough." He points to me. "This one's dad was a piece of work. He wanted us all to work together. Just because he knocked up a Hunter, he thought we could *coexist*—as if evil doesn't run through you monsters' veins." He snaps his fingers as if a thought just came to his head. "You know what my dad told me? I guess they used you as bait to murder your parents." He laughs. "Full circle, huh? Now, I'm using you to kill the next Human Liaison. I guess you're the most accomplished Hunter after all, Red—whether you like it or not."

I don't know if I believe Jack about the Hunters using me for my parent's death. I don't doubt it, but it's not something I can focus on now, even if the pain of his comment sears deep into my soul. "Jack, you can't murder us. The police will retaliate," I say in a calming voice, fully aware that Jack isn't in his right mind.

"Oh, I'm not going to murder you, my sweet. Remember? You need to produce me an heir. I'm just debating whether I should mutilate him now and keep him alive to watch you carrying my offspring or if I should end it now."

Jesus Christ, he's off the deep end. I think back to my reporter classes about dealing with mentally unstable interviewees.

"I'll fucking end you!" Cameron barks. "Try keeping me alive and see what happens."

I grab Cameron's hand, trying to calm him. That's not happening. We're finding a way to resolve this.

"So, what's the plan, Jack? What are we doing next?" I ask, keeping the panic from my voice.

"That's what I'm trying to figure out." He raises both of his arms as if physically weighing two options. "Kill him now or later."

"Jack, I need you to breathe. You're not thinking clearly."

Jack takes a big inhale of breath.

Although I was trying to calm him and de-escalate the situation, I didn't expect it to work. I try again. "I need you to put down the knife. I don't want you to hurt yourself."

"What?" Cameron whispers from behind me.

Jack walks to the countertop and places the knife down.

Cameron and I turn our heads to share a glance. I read his eyes, and he understands what I'm thinking. But is it possible? He nods to confirm.

I take a deep breath, focusing my attention on my words. "Jack, you need to take our handcuffs off."

Jack's gaze drills into mine. He doesn't move; he just watches me from the kitchen counter. I try again. "Jack, come over here and unlock our chains."

He steps toward me, the veins in his neck straining and his eyes darting back and forth. "That's right. Keep coming. Let us free."

He moves quicker, his boots pounding against the wood floor as he gets closer until he reaches us and kneels, digging in his pocket to retrieve the handcuff key.

Power rushes through my veins. I'm doing this. I'm controlling Jack with my mind. He might think I'm not powerful enough because of how little werewolf blood runs through my veins, but he's wrong. I don't know how, but I can control minds, even while locked in silver chains.

Cameron chuckles. "God, I love you," he says as Jack removes his handcuffs. Cameron pulls his arms free and examines his wrists.

My heart swells. I don't know if he means it seriously, but it's the first time he's said it. Sure, we're mates—destined for each other, but love—love is a choice. In this moment, I know I love him. It's crazy and so fast, but I know.

It happens quickly. I must have focused too much on Cameron's words and lost my hold on Jack's mind. I struggle against my chains, straining my neck to see what's happening behind me. All I can hear is skin against skin and heavy breathing. "Jack, stop!" I yell, but it's too late. I can't reach him anymore; his rage makes it too slippery to sink in my talons.

Jack's hands are around Cameron's throat, but the struggle only lasts momentarily. The change happens in an instant. The chair snaps underneath Cameron from his new weight and power.

Granny wakes from beside me, shrieking as she witnesses Cameron in his werewolf form, sinking his teeth into Jack's jugular, blood spraying from his mouth and gurgling his screams.

37

BIG BAD WOLF

I can't take my eyes away from his bloodied body. Cameron hasn't left my side, his hands shifting from my shoulder to my waist to my back as he speaks with the police. At first, I think I'm numb—the shock of watching someone I loved for so long die right before my eyes. But it's not that. I search every corner of my heart, trying to find a feeling, but there's nothing. I did love him, but after everything that happened—that love is like a wilted rose—only the thorns remain.

A small part of me feels sorry for him. He'd spent his life brainwashed by his psycho father and their cult, but he threatened to rape me and kill my mate. How could I feel sorry for him? How else could this have ended without living a life in fear? I'm not angry at Cameron, although I'd rather him not have murdered Jack in Granny's kitchen—he didn't have a choice.

"Ma'am, we have some questions," the police officer knocks me out of my trance in a tone that suggests this isn't the first time he's said this to me. I tear my eyes away from Jack as they cover him with a black sheet and turn my attention to Sergeant Brick, wearing a linen-pressed suit, his badge on his lapel, his smokey eyes pinning me in place.

"What?" I say, crossing my arms over my chest.

Cameron inches closer to me, wrapping his hand tightly around my hip.

Sergeant Brick clears his throat. "I need you to tell me what happened here?"

"Why? So you can pretend that it didn't happen and that the werewolves are to blame?"

Brick sighs, flipping open the small notepad he removed from his front pocket. "My job is to examine the evidence. Can you help me do that?"

I throw my arm in the direction of the three chairs and the chains sitting on the floor before bringing my marked wrists up to my face. "Is this not enough evidence that Jack went crazy and strapped us—including my little old Granny to chairs and threatened our lives? Jack was strangling Cameron and threatened to rape me."

"I see, ma'am, but your Grandmother has no recollection of the events, and I can't just take Mr. Badson's word for it."

I glance over at Granny, sitting at the kitchen table, the paramedics shining a light into her eyes. Granny woke up when Cameron ripped Jack's throat out, but in only a few seconds, she completely forgot what happened or that she was tied up. I should be thankful she won't be weighed down with the gore and trauma of it all, but my heart aches that she'll never remember what really happened to her daughter, and I'll never be able to share a part of myself—my werewolf part—with her.

I sigh, pull the tape recorder out of my pocket, and press the replay button. Jack's voice sounds around us. "Oh, I'm not going to murder you, my sweet. Remember? You need to produce me an heir. I'm just debating whether I should mutilate him now and keep him alive to watch you carrying my offspring, or if I should end it now." I turn it off. "Is that good enough for you?" I ask plainly.

"We're going to need that for evidence," Brick says, reaching for the tape recorder.

I hand it to him. "Don't worry; everything is automatically uploaded to the Cloud. If this whole incident isn't taken seriously, I will share it with someone above your pay grade. I work for the New York Times, remember? I know how to get the word out."

Brick sighs. "We're on your side. Navigating between the Hunters, the Weres, and the general public is much more difficult than you think. We're operating in secrecy and amid a century-old rivalry." He holds the tape recorder up to me. "This is good. This is what we need to put important people away—to keep people safe. But we're going to need more."

"More?" Cameron speaks up, his voice lined with anger.

"Well, would you happen to have recorded details about the Hunter's meeting place, names of the people involved in the murder of your parents and the people in the clearing, and information on future plans?"

Cameron and I exchange a look. I'd been hoping to get Jack to admit to all of that, but the only person he incriminated was himself and his dead father, and they won't be a problem for anyone else anymore. I shake my head.

Brick leans in. "I've been trying to get the National Department of Supernatural to take the Hunters more seriously as a terrorist group since I got into my position, but all I've been able to gather as evidence is he said, she said, and dead bodies with no evidence leading to their murders. This is something." He smiles, tapping the tape recorder to his temple.

I've never heard of the National Department of Supernatural, but I guess I've got much more to learn about my "werewolf-ness."

"I'm glad you're in town, Ms. Hoodson. I hope we will work together soon. I'm glad you're one of us." He winks before turning away on one heel and walking toward the group of police officers conversing in the corner.

I turn to Cameron. "One of us? Does that mean..."

Cameron shrugs, eyeing Brick. "I don't know. I've never seen him at a Council meeting, and he's never mentioned anything to me. He was transferred to our town around the same time I became the Liaison." Cameron shakes his head, turning to me. "I always thought he didn't care about Weres, but maybe I'm missing something."

I replay Sergeant Brick's words even as I try to use Cameron's dark eyes to distract me.

This is just the beginning... I'm glad you're in town, Ms. Hoodson.

My work isn't finished here. There's nothing for me to report back to the Times about the attacks unless I want to expose myself, my family history, and the man I love most, putting us more at risk. I probably don't have a job after weeks of radio silence, but do I care anymore? The answer comes to me before I even have time to contemplate. *No.* My life is here now, with Cameron—my mate.

I pick up my wrists. "Well, I guess we're not getting put in handcuffs and sent to jail just yet."

He nods, pulling me into him and resting his head between my head and shoulder. "Good, I'm tired of being locked up."

I pull back. "You? This is my fourth time being kidnapped since I got into town."

He tilts his head as if weighing the thought. "Touche."

I place my hands on his shoulders. "Besides, I enjoyed the last time you were chained to a poll. I wouldn't mind reliving that again."

"Ms. Hoodsman," he whispers in a low growl. "Naughty girl." He spanks my ass slightly and nips at my neck.

My core heats, and I close my eyes to revel in his touch. We're safe. Cameron's alive, Granny's alive.

Granny.

I pull away. "I need to check on Granny."

Cameron nods, and I walk away from him, stopping and turning once I sense he's not following me.

He stands where I left him, rubbing at his arm, his expression unsure.

"Are you coming?" I ask.

"Oh, yeah." His face brightens. "I just didn't know if you wanted time alone with her."

I grab his hand. "You're my mate. I want you to meet my Granny."

He smiles and leans in to kiss me on the lips, nipping me with transformed teeth before pulling away.

I place my hands on his chest. "Just put the fangs away, at least until after Granny decides she loves you."

He smirks. "I don't know. Wolves sure do have an appetite for little old Grannies."

38

CRIMSON WOLVES

"Are you sure this isn't over the top?" I ask as Cameron opens the passenger-side door, his face warming up into a full grin. "Are you kidding? You look fucking fantastic," he says, extending his hand to me.

I roll my eyes. "Well, I know that, but I'm wearing a ball gown." I stare at my red floor-length dress as I shift my weight to Cameron. He wraps his arm around me, twirling before setting me on the ground. "And I'm wearing a tux."

I look over his shoulder at the building behind him. "Is this the Moose Lodge?"

"Where else would we have a banquet in Dayton?"

I smack his arm. "Cameron! I am most certainly overdressed!"

"I think you look delicious. I could swallow you whole." He plants a kiss on my exposed shoulder.

I grunt with a smile. "Let's just get this over with." I walk toward the entrance, dragging Cameron behind me.

He pulls me backward. "On second thought, let's just go home. I don't know if I can wait hours to get you out of that dress."

"Cameron!" I stop, spinning to face him and slap his chest. "There are people!" I look around to assess who's nearby. If I thought I was overdressed before, now I'm worried we're completely out of line. Cloaked figures pass by, making their way toward the entrance.

I turn to Cameron, confusion riddled across my face.

"Their identities are a secret, remember? I'm the only one who's known by the public."

"So I will be in a red ball gown, and everyone else will be in dark cloaks? Got it. Let's go home." I start toward the car, but Cameron grabs my wrists. "Once they make it through security, they'll de-robe. I can't promise everyone won't be staring at you, but it won't be because they're displeased with your outfit. Maybe jealous, but I promise you look perfect."

I grunt. "Fine, but only because it took me like an hour and a half to do my hair."

He kisses my lips, and I wipe the red lipstick off his face before we turn and head toward the front door.

Two burly men in black suits and dark sunglasses stand at the front, their arms crossed over their chests. They nod, moving to the side and opening the door for us. "Cameron, Mildred, welcome."

"It's just Red," I call over my shoulder as we step inside. They ignore me.

"Wow." I gasp as we step into the banquet hall. Candlelight illuminates white linen tables covered in red roses. A string quartet plays in the corner of the room. Waiters in fitted suits pass around glasses of champagne on silver trays. I peer at the attendees entering, shedding their cloaks and handing them to the coat check at the front of the room. My nerves about being overdressed melt away until we walk further into the room, every head turning toward me.

"Um, should I be worried I will end up in a werewolf prison again?" I ask, not lifting my gaze from the people around me but folding into Cameron.

He laughs, taking my hand and kissing my knuckles. "News travels fast in the werewolf community. Nobody can stop talking about the newcomer who killed one of the most dangerous Hunters."

"But I didn't kill him," I whisper.

"I mean, your powers did most of the work. Besides, I didn't think it would hurt to embellish the details of your victory to the board members. You did escape their prison, remember? You needed some points in your favor."

"Ms. Hoodsman." A handsome man in his forties with dark hair and a clean-shaven face appears before us. "I'm glad to see you could make it to our Blood Moon Banquet tonight." He extends his hand. "I'm Minister Grimm."

"Nice to meet you," I say, flashing a smile and shaking his hand.

"Oh, we've already met," he says before sipping his champagne.

A waiter comes from my side and offers me a drink. I grab it, thank him, and take a sip before addressing Grimm. "We have?"

"I must admit, it's not the best circumstances to meet our new Lady Liaison by throwing her in a dungeon. My apologies, but I promise we would have given you a fair trial if you had only waited until after the Blood Moon. The time leading up to it can get a bit *hairy* for us—we don't always act most rationally." His cheeks heat.

I offer a soft smile. I can't be too angry since I understand what he's saying. There was no way I could have controlled my primal needs on that Blood Moon night, and I wasn't fully into my powers yet. Goosebumps pepper my skin as I think about that night, and I lean into Cameron, who grabs my arm and squeezes it as if he can read my mind. He can't. I'm still the only one who seems to have that power, although I've only been able to demonstrate it during sex with Cameron. Maybe with more fucking it would become more powerful. There's only one way to test it.

"May I introduce you to my nephew, Jeremy." Grimm's words knock me back to the moment.

"Hello," the freckled teenager says with a wave. His eyes shift nervously.

"Hey! I know you!" I exclaim with a laugh. His shrill voice puts me right back in that dungeon. "Sorry about tricking you. I hope you didn't get too much heat." I say, slapping his arm.

The boy's face reddens, but his uncle speaks for him. "We cut him a break since his brain wasn't working fully due to the Blood Moon. We're just happy that it's over, and we are all back to our full, cognitively functioning selves. That's what this Banquet is to celebrate—the end of the Blood Moon."

"Gotcha."

Grimm sighs. "Well, I'll let you two get back to your night. Enjoy yourselves, and thank you both for all you've done to keep our people safe."

I smile, and he turns to walk away but stops, turning on his heel. "Oh, Ms. Hoodsman. I was a friend of your father. I know he would be so proud of you. I can't wait to see what you do next here in Dayton."

My eyes well, and I nod, biting back my tears. Cameron spins me around, taking the champagne glass from my hand and placing it on a nearby tray. He studies my eyes. Understanding fills his own before he leans in to kiss me softly. "Dance with me." He doesn't give me time to answer, wrapping one hand around my waist and leading me with the other.

I giggle as I fall into step, resting my head on his shoulder and breathing in the smell of him—the smell I could bathe in.

My eyes trail around the room, catching the faces of people I swear I've seen my whole life. There's the butcher. There's the lawyer with his face plastered over every park bench. I pop my head up. "Carmen's here!" She's wearing an emerald-green dress and looks breath-catchingly beautiful.

I wave to her, and once her eyes meet mine, she squeals and barrels toward us. "If it isn't my kinky brother and his mate!" she yells, slapping Cameron on the back.

Cameron releases me, his eyes hardening and his voice in a harsh whisper. "Would you keep it down!"

"Calm down, lover boy. No one cares what weird prisoner roleplay games you both enjoy."

Cameron huffs, and I can't help but giggle. God, I can't wait to watch her get under his skin and bring him back to his childlike self more often. "Hey, we weren't roleplaying. I was very much his prisoner, and you abandoned me." I push her arm. "So much for girl code."

She waves away the notion. "Yeah, yeah. I could see what was about to happen. Don't act like you didn't appreciate me leaving you with your mate once you gave in. Clearly, you're here with him tonight on your own accord, but if he's still trapping you, just say the word. I'd pick you over him any day."

"Hey!" Cameron whines.

"Oh, you know I'm only kidding, big bro." She pinches his cheeks. "Well, sort of. Not really." She pats his chest, her eyes scanning around the ballroom. Her brows furrow. "Excuse me, I just saw an annoying pest I must attend to." She places her champagne glass down and marches toward the other side of the room. She takes a few steps before turning back to us. "Oh, Red, let's get coffee this weekend, okay? Love ya!" she says before twirling away.

I trail her, watching as she plants herself in front of an enormously tall gentleman wearing a grey suit. She points her finger at him, not caring that she's yelling at the man in a room full of people. He rolls his eyes and looks down at her with disdain. Wait. I know that man.

"Sergeant Brick?"

Cameron nods. "I invited him. I thought it would be good for him to see our community. For him to understand we're people, not just monsters." He pulls me close to him again, swaying me to the music.

"So is he...."

"I don't know. I can't sense it off him."

I place my head back on his shoulder. "Well, I guess it's good to have the police on our side now. Even if Carmen and him don't get along."

Cameron picks up his gaze to watch the two fighting before laughing and shaking his head. "Hopefully, she doesn't scare him away."

"I don't know. I think he likes it." I watch as he looms over her, his gaze flicking from her lips to her eyes.

I sigh. "Hopefully with the cops on our side, it will mean the end of the Hunters."

"I doubt that."

"Why?" I furrow my brow, meeting his eyes.

"It's going to mean a lot of work. We've been in the shadows for too long. It's time we show people who we are and that we can't be erased. Besides, your mother was a Hunter. People's minds can be changed."

I nod. He's right.

An idea pops into my head. It involves me staying here and using my reporter skills to give my people a voice. The idea doesn't scare me anymore. Dayton and Cameron are my home. "I think I know how I can help."

Cameron smiles. "I knew you would." His eyes trail my lips, and all my plans dissipate from my mind. He presses his body closer to me, and our dancing becomes more of a sway. He leans into my ear. "What was I thinking letting you leave the house like this without being properly fucked. How am I supposed to survive this night?"

I smile, whispering into his ear. "Maybe shmooze some more council members. That should get your mind off it."

His grip tightens around me. "No, I can't wait." His breath is hot against my neck. He pulls away from me, grabbing my arm. "Follow me."

I don't have time to protest as he drags me toward the opposite end of the banquet hall. We turn a corner after the bathrooms, and Cameron wiggles the handle of a utility closet, swinging it open and pushing me inside.

I trip back, catching myself on the shelves as he shuts and locks the door behind him, hurriedly peeling off his coat and white button-down. It's dark, but my eyes quickly adjust to his form before me from the strip of light at the bottom of the door.

"Cameron, people could hear us!" I keep my voice low as I push him away.

He presses forward, covering my mouth and leaning to my ear. "Then stop talking and fuck me. I promise I'll be quiet."

Arousal rolls through me at his orders, his tight grip, and the urgency as his hands palm my breasts over my dress. He removes his hand from my mouth, and I gasp for air, rolling my shoulders back and letting my thin straps fall.

"Good girl, giving yourself to me like I know you want to. I bet your cunt is already dripping." He hikes up my dress, grinning on my lips. "Not wearing any panties? Dirty little, Red."

I moan, unable to control myself, and his hand slaps back over my mouth. "Are you sure you don't want people to hear? Do you want an audience, little one?"

I reach for him, trying to unbuckle his jeans, needing him more than I need the air he's currently cutting off.

"Slow down. I'm not finished with you." He swats my hand away, bunching up the rest of my dress, and grabs my legs. "Hold on," he says, giving me just enough time to grab the shelf behind me as he brings my legs over his shoulder, his hot mouth at my core. "Oh fuck." He growls, breathing me in. "So good."

His fur brushes against my thigh, and I look down to see his face has transformed, a beast between my legs. His tongue darts out through his fangs, running along my seam. It's warm and rough, sending shivers down my spine as he pushes deeper, lapping me up with increased effort.

I lean into him, jerking my hips as he plunges his tongue inside of me. The sensation teases me, making me desperate for his cock—his knot. "Cameron, fuck me," I beg, but he just tightens his grip, grunting as he slides his long tongue to my clit.

His eyes bore into mine, and I notice blood coating his fur. "Oh my God, is that my blood." My cheeks heat—wholly embarrassed, and I strain to pull away, but his nails slightly turn into claws as he holds on tighter to my legs, not letting up on his grip. The pain mixes with the pleasure of his tongue—the thought of him enjoying the taste of me so much that he doesn't even care that I'm menstruating.

I focus my powers, tuning into his thoughts. Pleasure doubles inside of me. He's enjoying this as much—if not more than I am. I've never felt so wanted—so desired. He doesn't care what state he takes me in. I can't hold back any longer—my body shutters, folding in on itself like melted butter. He doesn't bring his mouth away from me until my body stills.

He only gives me a moment before gripping my ass and directing me to flip over. I don't hesitate, turning back to catch a glimpse as he frees himself from his slacks, gripping his length and lathering himself in the precum that's formed on his tip. His muzzle is covered in my blood, his face fully animal, and his fur trailing over his shoulders and pecs. I brace myself as he positions at my entrance.

He thrusts himself into me, and I cry out, completely forgetting about keeping quiet. His body folds over me, his face back to his human, clean-shaven form. "So loud and so tight," he murmurs into my ear. "You need to be quiet, or the other wolves will find you." He doesn't stop his strokes, pounding into my cunt from behind.

"My God!" I cry, my body tightening around him, my second orgasm crashing around me.

"That's right. Your god is here, fucking you—worshiping you." He grunts before pulling himself out of me, pumping his cock as he comes over my ass.

"Cameron," I gasp, looking back at him. "I wanted you to come inside of me."

He picks up a cardboard box beside him, removes a clean white rag, and wipes himself off me. "I know, but we have a party to get back to. We couldn't go back out on the dance floor with my knot engorged inside of you." He takes another rag, wiping the blood from me.

I turn around, glimpsing his knot growing, wishing it was inside of me. My mouth waters. I bring my eyes to his, his stare hungry as he wipes the blood—my blood from his face. He stalks toward me, leaning down to capture my lips. "You're disappointed."

"It just seems like such a waste," I murmur into his lips.

He chuckles. "A waste? I promise, my mate, there's much more where that came from."

I wrap my arms around him, pulling back and yawning. "I don't know about you, but this party is getting awfully boring."

"Oh, I agree." He smiles, putting my straps back over my shoulders. "I mean, look at this place." He motions to the supply closet around him. "What a dump."

"Yeah. We should just leave now."

"Yes, definitely." He kisses my lips. "I love you."

"I love you too," I murmur, barely removing my lips from his.

We slip out of the closet and slide through the back door, laughing and stumbling as we run to his truck.

39

THEY'D BE HAPPY

"Carmen, were you able to finish that puff piece about Danny's Groceries?" I ask, my laptop bag over my shoulder as I peek into her cubicle.

"Just finishing it now, boss. It will be on your desk by the end of the day."

I tap her wall. "Great, thank you! I'm having lunch with Granny, but I'll be back later."

Her words catch me before I turn to walk away. "Oh, next time you see my brother, tell him I need him to stop by the police station."

"Why?"

"I've been trying to get a statement from the police about the attacks, but Sergeant Brick is being a dick, but I guess what's new." She huffs.

"He won't comment at all?"

"Nope. It's like he's back to pretending that nothing happened."

I twist my lips. "That's weird."

"Yeah, I don't think we should have trusted him to go to the banquet. I have a bad feeling about him."

My stomach twists. Our plan for opening the Dayton Daily was to report on the real news happening in Dayton. We didn't plan to publicly release everything about werewolves and all their identities at once but bring to light the atrocities of the Hunters. We figured more werewolf identities would be revealed over time, but we couldn't keep hiding; it wasn't saving anyone. But if Sergeant Brick was double-crossing us now—that could be a problem.

"I'll tell him to head there and see what's going on when I get home tonight."

"Thanks," Carmen says, already turned to her computer and clicking through windows on her screen.

I push through the glass doors, turning and walking backward to see the new sign above my small office. "The Dayton Daily." I smile, letting the accomplishment wash over me. In only three months, I've rented this office space, secured printing and distribution, hired Carmen, and have a full-fledged local paper in operation. I've been so busy opening this thing and moving my life from New York to Cameron's cabin that I've barely stopped for a moment to appreciate it.

I resigned from my job at the Times. I thought I'd be sad once I sent my letter of resignation. My job was my life, but the second I hit that send button, I felt nothing but happiness. Now, here I am in front of my own paper. I take one last inhale of victory before jumping in my car and heading to Granny's.

***

"Is that you, Red?" Granny calls as I shut the front door behind me.

"Yes, and you're lucky. You need to keep your door locked. A monster could barge in."

"Funny you should mention me," Cameron calls as I enter the kitchen. He lies on the kitchen floor, his head underneath the sink.

Granny sits at the kitchen table, sorting through an old box filled with photos and papers.

"Granny, are you stealing my man?" I ask as I make my way to Cameron and stand over him. He rolls out from the shadows, grinning at me with a grease-stained face. "Are you here to gobble up my little ol' Granny?" I ask, falling to my knees and leaning over to kiss him.

Cameron wraps his arms around me, his lips grazing my ear as he whispers, "No, but I had hoped that helping fix your Granny's sink would win me some brownie points so I could gobble you up later." He nips my bottom lip.

My cheeks flush, and I push my body against him.

"Red, come over here. I want to show you something," Granny calls, her back turned to us.

I pop up, repressing the rosiness to my cheeks. "Yes, Granny." I pull out the seat beside her, leaning over to examine the papers in her hands. "What do you have there?"

"After you and I talked yesterday, you got me thinking. There are a lot of gaps in my memory of your parents. I remembered I had this box in the attic full of memories over the years. I thought it might help put together some of the pieces."

"Oh yeah?" I look to Cameron, now standing and wiping off his hands.

Over the past three months—between moving and building the local paper—I've been focusing on improving my powers. Fortunately for me, training involves a lot of sex with Cameron—each time, my powers heightened. Claws, super strength, mini-earthquakes, mind reading, and mind control are the extent of my powers, but they grow stronger daily. I couldn't only test them in the bedroom or when I was in life-threatening situations, so I decided to start practicing on Granny. I wasn't interested in reading her mind, but I hoped I could help restore the missing pieces and repair the damage the Hunters did to her.

After three months of no progress, I was about to call it quits, but last night something changed. She remembered her Hunter heritage. She remembered my father being part werewolf. It wasn't much, just the seed of the idea. I'd hoped I could build on it and uncover more. It seems like my hopes have come to fruition. Now, she's examining her missing memories all on her own.

I can't erase the smile on my face. My powers are growing, and I'm using them to help one of the people I love most. "What did you find?" I ask.

She hands me a picture of my parents on their wedding day. My mom wears a beautiful white gown, not a wedding dress, just a flowy white dress that looks like she found it last minute. My dad holds her in his arms, gazing at her with so much love behind his eyes.

I take the picture. "They look so happy."

"They were. I wasn't happy about them coming together at first. He was a werewolf, for Pete's sake—the enemy."

Anxiety shoots through my veins at her words. I hadn't thought that she might only remember my parents before she accepted my father. Could I have done more damage to her than good?

Her words slice through my panic. "Your mother invited me to their courthouse wedding two hours before it started." She shakes her head. "I could have strangled her, but I decided to go. She was my only daughter, and I wouldn't have been able to live with myself if I missed her special day. When I saw your parents up there at the front of the courtroom—the love in their eyes—I knew I had been wrong. They were mates. How could I hold onto my hatred when I witnessed something so opposite to what I grew up believing?"

"Did you believe they were mates when she told you?"

Granny nods. "Yes, it was obvious to everyone. Your father became more powerful. That's what threw the Hunters through a loop. They started speculating that she had some werewolf DNA, but I knew she didn't. Their love was so powerful that it created their own rules. That's when I realized all the lies I had been taught. We weren't so different than werewolves. And then you came along and showed me how even more powerful your parents love could be." She pulls out an old picture of me swaddled in my mother's arms.

"My eyes!" I gasp, holding the picture closer, staring at my bright, glowing eyes.

Granny nods. "You showed your powers early on. Your parents tried everything to keep it a secret, but it got out. The Hunters wanted you for themselves, but when your parents refused... well, you know what happened from there." Tears fill her eyes.

I reach out to grab Granny's hand, my eyes welling with tears. Cameron stands behind me, placing a steady hand on my shoulder. I've never seen Granny so emotional before. Maybe bringing her memories back wasn't the best idea. Maybe I should have let her live the rest of her days in her ignorant bliss. But then I watch as she picks up another picture of me and my mother, her face lighting up.

"Here's when you first started walking." She hands it to me.

I can't help but smile as well, seeing my young mother look at me with such love. Maybe these memories are painful, but with the pain comes so much joy because love existed here. How sweet is it to experience such love that hurts so much when it's gone?

I flip the card over, surprised to find my mother's handwriting on the back.

Red taking her first steps–the strongest crimson wolf to live. Soon she'll be running all through Dayton, causing all sorts of havoc.

I laugh and hold it up to show my mate. He smiles and squeezes my shoulder.

I wish she could see me now. She'd be so happy watching me taking down Hunters, starting a paper to bring light to the corruption that has haunted this town for years, and being fucked into oblivion every night by my mate. Okay, maybe she wouldn't *love* to see that last one, but she'd be happy to know I'm happy.

Something in my heart swells, and I know that wherever they are, they're smiling down on me.

40

JUST THE BEGINNING

I sip my hot cocoa, allowing the steam to seep into my pores before turning to the last page of my book. I've been so transfixed in the story—some fluffy enemies-to-lovers romance novel—that I haven't even noticed how much time has passed. The orange sun melts through the window next to the fireplace. The logs crack, the light dim and almost burned out. A chill has seeped into the cabin, and I pull my sweater closer. "Cameron?" I call, swiveling my head, but I don't see him.

I close my book and stand on my socked feet, shuffling across the hardwood floor. A loud bang sounds from outside, and I open the front door to see if it could possibly be my long-lost mate.

Sure enough, Cameron stands at the chopping block, swinging an axe overhead before smashing it down on an impressively large log. He's shirtless—of course, because there's never been a moment in our year together that he doesn't miss a moment to show off. I can't say I mind as I watch the intricate muscles in his abdomen flex with each swing. His biceps strain as he pulls the axe over his head again, grunting as sweat trickles down the side of his temple. I bet he smells heavenly, like musk and sex. I put my hand over my heart as I watch him, resisting the urge to run out in the snow and tackle him where he stands.

Okay, maybe I'm not the best at resisting urges. I only watch for a few more seconds before I take off, running to him as if a monster is chasing me.

He catches sight of me mid-swing, smirking through a heavy breath as he lets the axe fall to his side. He doesn't have time to brace himself before I barrel into him, wrapping my legs around his waist and bringing him to the snowy earth.

I pepper kisses down the side of his cheek as he tries—barely—to push me off him. "What are you doing?" he asks through a laugh. My lips meet his, but I only kiss his teeth since he smiles so big.

"I'm in a mood," I say between kisses. His body is warm under me, slick with his sweat.

"I see that." His hands rest on my ass. "I was trying to chop you some wood so you could continue to enjoy your book once the sun sets."

I pick myself up, hovering over him as I look down at him. "Please. You were out here looking all sexy and manly. You were practically *begging* me to jump you."

He shakes his head with a smirk. "Mrs. Badson, are you implying that I can't do normal activities without being turned into a sexual object."

I bite my lip, looking at the sky as if sorting through my thoughts. "Yes, but only for me, and only when I'm in heat." I press my body against him, capturing his lips, but he doesn't let me and breaks out into a laugh. "You're in heat? What does that mean?"

I kiss down his neck. "Well, I assume I'm ovulating based on what the sight of you does to my body, but since I'm a werewolf now, I guess I'm in heat."

Cameron wraps his arm around me and flips me over. The quickness of his movement takes the air from my lungs. "You know how I love it when you refer to yourself as a dog." He rolls his eyes, even if his smile betrays him.

"What can I say? I got that dog in me." I shrug.

He shakes his head and tsks. "You are just so charming." He leans in for a kiss, which I greedily accept.

I pull away. "Now, what more do I have to do to get you to fuck and breed me?"

He stills, his eyes glued to mine. "Breed you?"

I nod, biting my lip.

"Are you being serious?"

I grab his hand and shove it down my pants into the wetness of my cunt. "Does this feel serious?"

He bites his lips, his eyes rolling to the back of his head. "Fuck, Red."

"Yes, that's right. Please fuck Red." I whisper into his ear.

I screech as he swoops me up from the ground, throwing me over my shoulder and charging toward his cabin. He smacks my ass, and I giggle. "Ah, help me!" I yell.

He stops. "What are you doing? Who do you want to help you?"

I shrug. "I don't know. Thought it would be fun to pretend."

He shakes his head before opening the door and stomping toward the bedroom, throwing me on the bed roughly. I crawl back to the headboard as I watch him rip off his belt and pull down his pants, crawling over me in only his grey boxer briefs. I can't miss his hard and impressive length as it brushes the inside of my legs.

I brace myself for his rough hands, to continue the cat and mouse game I'm so eager to play, but instead, his lips meet mine, and he kisses me so gently I could cry. He pulls back. "I love you, you know that?" His eyes gaze seep into mine, and I nod. "And I will love our child so much."

"I know." I smile, tears forming in my eyes.

"I will never get over how grateful I am for you. That you would even consider carrying a part of me inside of you." Now, his eyes cloud with tears.

I bring my hand to his cheek. "Oh, Cameron. I've been carrying a part of you inside of me from the moment we met."

He shakes his head, his eyes glowing with happiness before he captures my lips with his. The kiss grows deeper quickly, and I soak in every small movement of him against me. My mate. He's mine. He's here with me, and the rest of our lives is just beginning.

THANKS FOR READING

Thank you for reading! If you liked *The Crimson Wolf: A Red Riding Hood Love Story,* make sure to leave a review.

Want Carmen and Sergeant Brick's story?

House of Wolves: A Three Little Pigs Love Story
Where pigs play pretend, and wolves hunt, a dark secret is about to be exposed.

Carmen, a determined werewolf journalist at the Dayton Daily, is on a mission to expose the Hunters' sinister activities without compromising her kind's secrecy. When young female werewolves begin to vanish under mysterious circumstances, the werewolf council senses a deeper conspiracy and suspects a police cover-up.

Past relationships with Officer Straw and Wood make Carmen the best candidate to go undercover and infiltrate the police force. The piggish men prove ineffectual, leaving her with no choice but to turn to Sergeant Brick—a man she loathes.

Forced to seduce him to uncover the truth, Carmen is shocked to find a strange connection between her and Brick. As the danger intensifies, Carmen discovers that Brick is hiding beastly secrets of his own.

With higher stakes than ever, Carmen must navigate her growing feelings and the perilous world of werewolves and Hunters to uncover the truth. Can she trust Sergeant Brick, or will his hidden nature lead to her undoing?

House of Wolves can be enjoyed as a continuation of The Wolfish Love Stories or as a stand-alone.

Stay up to date on all things G.M. Fairy!